FIRE BREATHING REMY

Dragons of the Bayou

CANDACE AYERS

Lovestruck Romance Publishing, LLC

It's the night before Lennox Ledoux's wedding.
The most exciting day of her life, right?
Why is she picturing the steel bars of a cage slamming shut?

When a huge, red creature crashes to the ground a few feet away, she's the only witness.
When it transforms into a hot, naked guy, she's still the only witness.

Remy swears he and Lennox belong together.
And, boy, does she want to believe him.

But he's clearly drunk and delusional.
Besides, she can't get out of the wedding now.
Not with guests in town and the entire event paid for.
Can she?

Chapter One

LENNOX

Glancing across the table at my fiancé, I pondered, not for the first time, the huge step I was taking. Married. I wouldn't let myself think of it as a potential mistake, so I'd just taken to calling it a *huge step*. And huge it was. If I doubted that for a second, I needed only to take a quick peek around the room to clarify everything. The main dining room of *La Elizabeth* was packed with well-wishers that I barely knew while my close friends were seated along the wall—out on the fringes. If that didn't speak volumes about the *huge step* I was taking. *Had* taken. I'd accepted David's proposal months prior.

David smiled, the strain around his eyes barely showing. I doubted it would be obvious to anyone else. To the world, apart from my close friends, David Thibodeaux was the picture of success and prosperity— and wealth. Wealthy beyond imagination, he was the perfect soon-to-be husband.

He was. Really.

"Madam Ledoux, would you care for more Cabernet?" A waiter in white gloves, wearing a suit that was probably more expensive than the dress I had on, appeared by my side, his neutral expression a contradiction to the stressed look on David's face.

I smiled but shook my head. "May I switch to water?"

"Oh, Lennox, it's perfectly acceptable to let loose a bit tonight. It's the night before your wedding after all." My mother's unwelcome commentary from a few seats over intruded on my interlude with the well-dressed waiter. She was leaning toward me, a pointed look on her face. "You've decided against a bachelorette soiree, after all. A second glass of wine won't kill you."

Glancing up at the waiter, I gave a slight nod. No use arguing about trivialities. Not with my mother.

David, wearing his slick but charmingly crooked grin, elbowed me. "Are you sure about that, Lenni? We're in New Orleans, after all. If there was ever a place for a bachelorette party, this is it."

My friends, seated in the corner against the wood-paneled wall of the five-star establishment, were laughing, drinking, and having what looked like an all-around merry old time. When Margo noticed my stare, I had to bite my tongue to keep from giggling as she faked a dramatic gag. "I'm sure. Tomorrow's a big day. I should get a good night's sleep."

"Well, as for me, I'll have plenty of time to sleep when I'm dead." David elbowed his best buddy, Royce, next to him. "I'm painting the town tonight on my last night of bachelorhood."

I was sure he was. David was a big fan of "fun." My mother in law, whose gaze was set on David with the adoration of a mother who firmly believed the sun rose and set on her only son, hadn't a clue just how much of a fan of fun he was. Choosing to remain silent, I just smiled at him. He'd settle down eventually, my mother assured me. "Men are just wired that way," she'd often told me. And she would invariably go on with her defensive rant of David, how men are naturally a little more curious than women, fickler, have wild oats to sow, yada yada yada.

My mother was an old-school southern belle, with her own value system. I wasn't exactly sure where it came from, but her excuses for the poor behavior of men—my father included—were never ending. She had as many excuses as she had extra cans of hairspray stored under her bathroom sink for a rainy day. You know, that rainy day when all the hairspray might vanish, raptured up to God himself.

"Lenni has never been a big partier. She's always been so demure—a good girl." My mother, not one to offer compliments, especially to me, was uncharacteristically singing my praises to David's mother, Eleanor. "She'll make David the perfect wife."

"Yes." Eleanor's smile was as fake as the potted greenery on the walls. "And if not, there's always the prenuptial agreement."

My cheeks heated. The table grew quiet, and I felt everyone's stares on me. It was all I could do not to get up and run to the ladies' room. I'd already done that as a quickie escape twice in the past hour. Once more and everyone would think I had bladder issues. Or the runs.

What the hell was I doing? Making a huge mistake?

Margo was in the corner waving her hand in the air to get my attention. She mouthed the words "are you okay," and judging by the concerned look in her eyes, she was skeptical of my nod.

Dad blessedly came to the rescue by changing the subject and breaking the tension. "So, David, how did you select the honeymoon location? The islands of Georgia, didn't you say?"

David jumped in enthusiastically with both feet. "Yes, sir. The resort we'll be staying at is on an exclusive island. It has some of the best golfing this side of the Mason-Dixon. Of course, it's got shopping for Lenni, too."

A honeymoon at a golf course. Just what every girl dreams of. Oh, well, at least my new husband will enjoy himself. I put my fork down and picked up the second glass of Cabernet. Taking a sip, I fought a wince. I hated wine.

The saxophone player on the small stage at the front of the restaurant put his instrument aside and announced he'd be taking a short break. In the interim, speakers released a light jazz melody.

"What a wonderful idea, David," Eleanor patted her son on the arm like he was a pet. "Golfing is a fine form of physical exercise. And how kind of you to consider one with good shopping for your bride. The shops may have some nice things suitable for you, Lennox."

Suitable for me. She was making a veiled reference to the extra thirty pounds I carried in the form of jiggly curves. Larger breasts and hips meant that I looked a little rounder and fuller than her upper-crust ladies at the country club found appropriate. Even the baggy cardigan I wore couldn't hide the fact that I was not a woman prone to liposuction and diet pills.

"She's been eating healthier to make sure the dress fits perfectly. I'm certain she'll keep some of those extra pounds off," my mother, forever *un*helpful, added. "The poor girl was cursed with her grandmother's figure. Big boned. On Jack's side, of course. You knew my mother. She was as slender as a rail her whole life."

"Shelby was always that."

With impeccable timing, dessert was presented, large slices of sumptuous cheesecake drizzled with rich chocolate sauce and a mound of fresh raspberries with a side of beignets—New Orleans fritters— square pillows of dough deep fried and dusted with powdered sugar.

The smell was divine and almost rivaled by the presentation. My mouth watered, and Mom's lie about me eating healthier ricocheted around my head. A bead of sweat formed on my temple as I held my fork aloft, my stare boring into the beckoning confection.

"Lenni?" My mother's voice held both a clean directive and a stern warning. Put the fork down. Just say no. You're too big already. Impress your soon-to-be in-laws by showing them you're at least trying.

I dropped the fork. "If you'll please excuse me, I'm going to return this to the kitchen and see if perhaps they might have a healthier substitute." It was not worth the disapproving glares to contradict my mother, especially in front of my new in-laws, and I had a strong impulse to get away from her, from all of them, if only for a few minutes.

"Really, Lenni, you're not a waitress." David shook his head and laughed as though I was an incorrigible child. "You must learn to let the wait staff do their jobs. You're soon to be a Thibodeaux, honey."

Silently, striving to not draw attention to myself, I stood clutching my dessert plate of decadent perfection. "It's no big deal. I need to get a quick breath of fresh air, anyway. I think someone might be smoking close by. You know, my asthma."

"You have asthma?"

I was already walking away. No, I didn't have asthma, but what I *did* have was a hankering to devour the cheesecake and beignets without starting a third world war. As I passed Margo's raised brows on the way to the kitchen, I shook my head at her unspoken offer to come along. It was imperative that I was as inconspicuous as possible or my mother would scent me out like a bloodhound.

Slipping between the swinging double doors that led to the kitchen, I offered an apologetic face as I swiped a fork. The nearest prep cook pointed me to the exit. Ah, sweet escape.

REMY

"You're sure you're in shape to fly home?" Chyna spoke to me then frowned at Blaise, no doubt communicating her thoughts to him tele-pathically, if her silent but penetrating expression was any indication. "I've never seen one of you dragons so drunk. He's Cherry-summer-of-2009 wasted."

Cherry lifted her head from the couch and glared at her twin. "We agreed never to talk about that."

Blaise clapped me on the back. "My brother has always known his limit. Plus, spirits do not affect our kind the way they do humans. We are *dragons!*"

I released a fearsome roar. Why did it emerge sounding more like a pathetically whiny whimper? Must be the acoustics in the room. When my head swiveled and the room spun, I worried that I'd imbibed a little more than I realized. Not that it mattered. I was never out of control. Expressing that statement to the room, I stood up. With a minor sway, I bowed gallantly and backed toward the exit.

"Watch out for the—"

The backs of my knees hit something and I flew backward. Hard. My large frame contacted the ground with a thud, and my mind reached to assess the situation.

"Pack-n-Play..." Cherry finished quietly, with a snicker. "Watch out for the Pack-n-Play is what I was trying to say."

Cezar stood over me, looking down with a smartass smirk on his face. "Brother, you squished the youngling apparatus."

I glanced around and frowned when I saw that I was inside the cage they'd bought for their coming young. "What was that doing behind me?"

Blaise helped me up, laughing. "Now I am beginning to worry about your flying skills, bro."

I sidestepped the crumpled cage and grasped the arm of the sofa to steady myself and prove that it was the cage's fault, not mine. I was fine. "I will be making my exit now."

A chorus of goodbyes followed us as Cherry walked me to the door. "You're welcome to stay the night in the guest room, Remy."

"No, thank you."

"Be careful, okay?" Her expression, a mixture of concern and pity, prompted me to weave my way out the door and down the dock faster.

A minor misstep landed me with a splash in the water off Cezar's dock. I emerged from the murky depths with an ungraceful sputtering cough and shifted right then and there to avoid any more concerned looks from Cherry, or offers to remain among the mated crowd. Chyna had also pulled me aside earlier in the night to whisper encouragement as she knew how it was to be the single twin of a newly mated sibling.

I shot into the night sky too fast and too high and did a few unintentional acrobatic maneuvers before I was able to balance myself. Steadying my dragon, who was just as forlorn as I was, proved challenging. Still, I managed to pilot myself in the general direction of home.

The evening had been punishing. We dragons tended to be solitary for the most part, but humans, on the other hand, not so. Cherry, Chyna, and Sky loved to host gatherings for no good reason at all. Fine. But Chyna and Blaise continually nagged me to attend their get-togethers, as they called them. I was happy for my brother and my friends. They'd found their mates and were living life to the fullest. The three of them, Blaise, Cezar, and Beast, were happier than I'd ever seen them. Even Cezar, whose pregnant mate was uncomfortable and as prickly as a cactus lately, strutted around grinning from ear to ear.

My formerly dark, brooding brother had grown so exuberant he resembled a clown with his broad grin.

It wasn't easy being one of the unmated loser dragons, and it was especially difficult to be the only loser in attendance at the mated-crowd get-togethers. Three of us were left, as yet unmated, to worry about the upcoming eclipse. Without a mate, we would slowly go insane and would need to be put down for our own good and the safety of the world at large.

Neither the eclipse nor the looming threat of impending insanity was the source of my distress. It was watching Blaise with Chyna... I wanted that. A mate. To grin so big I looked like a clown. To have a female to make love to and hold in my arms all night long. That was the craving, the longing, and the hopelessness that was causing my anguish.

Yet, I still showed, the only mateless dragon at the party. Alone and lonely. Alone and bitter. Alone and intoxicated.

I was, without a doubt, inebriated and not exactly sure where I was. Headed in the direction of my castle, maybe. Nothing looked familiar. Possibly because there was two of everything. Doubles of every unfamiliar tree, unknown swamp, peculiar marsh, foreign road, and strange building.

Flying a little lower, I closed one eye. Surely, something would come into focus eventually. I only realized how high I'd been flying when I broke through the cloud cover and found myself on the edge of a city. Bright lights lit up like the humans' Christmas trees. Swirling, glowing, colorful—so pretty.

There were jazz melodies floating on air and spicy aromas of jambalaya and seafood gumbo. And, under the tantalizing scents and sounds, something else—something arousing—tickled the edges of my consciousness, luring me. I flew toward the enticements, hoping for maybe a big pot of Louisiana culinary specialties.

I hadn't noticed the brick wall until my head informed me of its presence by connecting with it. My balance faltered and everything blurred for a minute. Before I could right myself, I fell to the ground, dead weight. *Thud.* The clumsiest landing in history.

Lying there, groaning as the aches started, I evaluated the situation. How had I gotten so lost? Not sure. Had I just revealed the existence of my kind to a bunch of humans who couldn't keep secrets? Not sure. Was I dead, injured, or in an unconscious dream state? Not sure about that either.

Rolling over caused a growl to escape me. The ground hurt. Almost as much as the wall. I was a dragon, though. I was fine. Plus, that tickling, arousing sensation was still hanging around. Not the food. No, this had my dragon's scales up. It was slightly reminiscent of the sweet flowers that my mother had grown all those centuries ago. That's what I was smelling. Incomparable and delicate, the particular flower had been exceedingly rare.

How could it be here, in the new world?

LENNOX

I was minding my own business, leaning against the brick wall behind *La Elizabeth*, blissfully devouring my cheesecake with chocolate and raspberries and beignets, when a giant...*thing*...fell from the sky. I stood frozen for a while, waiting on someone else to check it out. I had no business snooping behind the row of hedges to my right. I had no business investigating what had fallen from the sky with a god-awful thud. I had no business trying to catch a glimpse of what was now over there grunting and groaning.

Mind your business, eat your cheesecake, go back inside, and pretend you chose to forgo the healthier dessert option in favor of abstinence. Finish the wretched rehearsal dinner. Go back to the hotel and get a good night's sleep. *That* was my business.

No one came, though. Perhaps no one else had seen or heard the thing fall. How that could be, I had no clue. It had been a spectacular fall. Crowds of pedestrians were walking by on the street, passing not too far away. The area was shadowed, but not enough for no one else to see nor hear *anything*.

I mouthed another bite of beignet and chased it with another bite of cheesecake before setting the plate down atop a large yellow post and moving toward the line of hedges. I knew better. I watched horror movies from time to time. If this were a movie, the audience would be shouting, *Don't do it! Don't go alone! Turn around! Run!*

Was I really going to walk the same path as one of those ditzy scream queens?

The hedges were tall, meant to hide the trash dumpster and delivery area on the other side. Still, I could see something jutting over them. Something large and deep red, and...scaly? Something so dark that I almost couldn't tell...that it was red with gold veins. *Veins?*

My internal shouts to myself to run for my life didn't reach my feet. Instead, my feet inched closer. My chest was fully pressed against the trimmed hedges, my face leaning in, straining to get a good peek between a gap. It had rained earlier, and I was sure my silk dress would be ruined by the droplets clinging to the shrubbery, but I couldn't help myself.

That must be how horror movie characters felt.

The mellow tone of a saxophone could be heard from the restaurant, reminding me I'd been "getting a breath of fresh air" for a while now. As I leaned in farther, the thing moved! Two giant wings, both deep crimson, repositioned, and the thing growled. It sat up, almost humanlike, with a giant head and two glowing, golden eyes. Then, like magic, or a bad acid trip, it vanished and in its place was seated a man. Stark naked.

The shock of it all threw me off balance, and I somehow managed to trip over my own feet and fall right through the small gap in the hedges. *Thud.*

Highly undignified and lacking poise and sophistication, as usual, I struggled and fought the branches of the bushes as they poked and prodded, grabbing at my dress and cardigan, snagging my hair and scratching my skin.

Managing to right myself, albeit on the other side of the row of hedges, my legs trembled like a newborn calf's. The naked man and I locked eyes. I held that gaze like my life depended on it.

Not knowing what to say to the beautiful man, I just stared. Do I ask if he saw a big red creature that crash landed? Do I pretend that I hadn't seen him transform into a very sculpted man from a...large, red bird? That is what I had seen, right? Wasn't it? Or, was it? My eyes gaped in amazement. My legs wouldn't move, but if I could have gained some control over them, maybe I should have had them walk me to the psych ward.

Despite my immobility, my body felt invigorated. As though I was plugged into a power source. Buzzing raw energy pulsed through me.

The naked stranger got to his feet and finger combed his hair. It was short on the sides, longer on top, bright red, and looked as soft as silk to the touch, even with the twigs and leaves in it. The grin that parted his lips was stunning—sparkling white teeth slicing a full beard and mustache, the same bright red shade as his hair. His eyes, though, oooh, the eyes. They were gold.

"Mate." His deep voice was gravelly, and the slight slur in his words suggested that he was a bit tipsy. Suggestion confirmed when he stepped toward me with a swaying, weaving gait. Dead giveaway. He was hammered.

Then, my eyes strayed. So many abs, so many muscles, so many... inches...holy cow! I slapped my hand over my eyes and turned away. "I am so sorry! I was just...I heard... Are you alright?"

"I must be dreaming. If I am, do not awaken me, goddesses." His husky whisper was right behind me, and his touch, a fingertip that ran down my arm, a feather-light caress that scorched a path like it was on fire, sent shivers up my spine.

My body's response was unlike anything I'd experienced, and I wasn't sure how to react. Not when my nipples pebbled and strained against the fabric of my bra, my pulse beat a rapid rhythm to my core, and my flesh dotted in goosebumps. I sucked in a breath of air that smelled like dark chocolate and pine forests. Mmm, the naked stranger smelled fantastic. No wonder my body was freaking out.

Over another man.

The day before my wedding.

If I wasn't so lost in the moment, in the unconventional experience and fresh, novel feelings, I would have been moving away. Running away. When his warm palms grasped my waist and turned me to face him, I should've backed away. When he pulled my body into his, I should've offered resistance. What the hell was wrong with me, allowing a strange man to touch me, to arouse me?

"So beautiful," he whispered. "You are so beautiful." He stared down with those glowing eyes. Mesmerizing. "What is your name, mate?"

"L-Lennox."

He leaned down, buried his face in the crook of my neck and inhaled. When his tongue stroked across my skin, I should have freaked out. I should not have shivered and grabbed onto him like a starving woman. Or let my head fall to the side. Or released a moan of pleasure. I should have proclaimed my almost-married status. I should have turned and walked away.

So many should haves and shouldn't haves.

"Your scent is provocative, seductive. You have captivated me, and I would spend forever right here, breathing you in, my mate. Lennox." Even though his speech was slurred, and a little oddly phrased, the sincerity behind his words was intense.

No business... I chanted to myself over and over. Go back inside. Go back to the hotel and change first. His hands, though. They stroked my lower back, one of them trailing lower. A low, guttural growl, and the presence of the steel rod between his legs that was suddenly pressing into my stomach, indicated he liked my curves. A lot.

A door slammed somewhere nearby, startling me back to reality. Prying myself away from him and putting some distance between us, granted me a glorious frontal view of the amorous but drunken naked guy. "Um... Where did you come from? You shouldn't be here at all, uh...*exposed.*"

His teeth dug into his bottom lip, he cocked his head, then eyed me through hooded lids. Oh, my, what was life doing to me?

"I...got lost. I must put clothes on. You are correct. This world has strict laws about clothing." He gestured down his body and then looked at mine with a hungry glint in his eyes. "I understand those laws to an extent. Covering my body, sure, but why a law to cover yours? That is a crime. A crime against..."

I couldn't help the giggle at his suggestion. Then, he hiccupped and lost his train of thought. "Where were you headed?"

"To my castle. Which is...it seems I took a wrong turn."

"Castle? Uh-huh."

His brow furrowed as he scanned the area before inhaling deeply through his nose. "I cannot smell anything with you so near. I cannot focus. You are the sweetest..."

"Do you need me to move away?"

"No. Do not move. I would rather remain lost in you."

I giggled again, shook my head, and grinned down at my dirt-smudged heels. "Do you know where we are?"

"I do not. I saw the sparkling city lights before I fell. So beautiful." His throat worked as he looked up, then studied my face dreamily. "They lit up the path and drew me here—to you."

"New Orleans." Ignoring his charm was not easy, but the guy needed to put on some clothes before he got himself arrested. I was also beginning to think he might have bumped his head on the way down. "Do you know what day it is?"

His wide, beaming smile lit up the night.

"The first day of our future together."

Chapter Four
LENNOX

The stranger needed help. He was obviously not in complete control of his faculties. Drunk off his ass and possibly concussed. It was hard to look past all the naked, tanned hotness and muscles, but I was strong. I could do it.

"Do you feel okay? Did you hit your head when you crash land—I mean, fell? Did you hit your head when you fell?"

He shrugged. "It will heal if I did."

I sighed. "Okay, we'll start smaller. What's your name?"

"Remy."

"Good. Your last name, Remy?"

"I do not have one. Just Remy." He inched closer to me. "Your dress is torn."

Glancing down at the mess that used to be my best dress, I bit my lip. Sure enough, in addition to the water spots, there were stains and tears. I opened my mouth to say something. I had no idea what, since the second my eyes met his heated gaze all coherent thoughts flew out of my addled brain. The way he was looking at me... Oh, no, no, no. The guy thought he was a "one-namer" like Madonna or Bono, or Drake. Regular, noncelebs had a last name. Plus, I was almost married.

"I'm going to need your last name if I'm going to find someone who can help you, Remy. Think hard."

He smiled at me, a small dimple showing in his left cheek just above his beard line. "I don't need someone to help me. I found you. You are everything I need."

I was in over my head. I took my phone out of the small pocket of my cardigan and shot off a text to Margo. I needed to call in the reinforcements, especially if I was going to take care of Remy without touching him inappropriately. "Friends of mine are going to come out and help us, okay? We need to get you inside and dressed. Then, we can get you to a doctor or find your people."

"You wish for your friends to see me naked?"

A sharp flash of anger and jealousy bolted through me, leaving me flushed and shaking my head. No, I did not. I shrugged off my cardigan and held it out to him. "Hold that over your, uh, man parts."

He held it over his chest and grinned. "Which parts, mate?"

So drunk. I crossed my arms over my chest and lowered my eyes to his still-hard erection. "Um... You should put that thing away."

"Put it away?" He looked genuinely confused. His bottom lip jutted out and his head tilted to the side slightly.

I groaned. "It's harder to cover you up if your sword is en garde, ready to fence with anyone who walks by."

The cardigan fell as he shook his head, stepped closer and held both sides of my neck, his thumbs caressing my throat. "Not *anyone*. Only you."

The way touched me, the way he had held me, even the way he was speaking to me and the words he used were everything I'd ever wanted. When I was a young girl who dreamed of the man who would sweep her off her feet, he was just the kind of dream man I envisioned. Except, back then he would have been clothed. He cupped my face with a tender, almost reverent touch and stared with fervor. Swallowing audibly, I squeezed my eyes shut. "Who are you?"

"I am Remy—your mate."

Approaching footsteps triggered my panic. I pulled away from him, somewhat in a daze, and stooped, attempting to snatch the cardigan from the ground at his feet. Margo cornered the row of hedges just in time to see me poke my eye right into Remy's impressive boner. I gasped and stumbled backward. Remy swore. I could hear a tinge of pain in his voice, but he reached out and grabbed my arm to steady me.

"That is one method of 'putting it away,' I suppose."

I laughed despite my embarrassment and the pain in my eyeball. Sheesh, what would it say about me if I blinded myself the night before my wedding on another man's penis?

Margo rushed forward clasping both my arms. "Who is this?"

I held up my free hand and waved her off. "He needs some help."

"He's *naked*." She swore, then her eyes traveled all the way down to his toes and back up. "Impressively naked."

"I am Remy. Lennox is my mate."

Margo hissed but otherwise remained silent. A small gasp caught my attention and, with my good eye, I noticed my other best friend, Nance, standing a few feet away with her jaw practically on the ground.

"Remy, please put the sweater over yourself."

Margo dug her fists into her hips. "Yeah, dude, cover your junk."

I had to bite my lip to keep from giggling. I seemed to have this hysterical giggling fit trying to get loose, for some reason. "Margo, Nance, this is Remy—no last name. I found him out here. He had quite a fall, and I think he hit his head. He needs some clothes."

"Well, he can't stand around out here. There are cops everywhere." Margo looked at me, then Nance. "Okay, make sure that cardigan stays over the python downstairs, and we'll form a human shield around him."

"He's huge," Nance piped up. "I don't know if that'll be sufficient."

I glared at Nance, suddenly very annoyed with her. "Really?"

She laughed. "I mean him, in general, Lennox. I'm not sure the three of us will be enough of a shield."

"We're going to have to be enough." I focused again on Remy, finding him happily grinning down at me. "We're going to take you somewhere safe and find you some clothes, okay?"

"As long as I am with you, I will be happy."

Margo coughed, and I elbowed her. Holding my breath, I attempted to tie the cardigan around Remy's nether region as best as I could, which resulted in me being face to butt and wondering how a man's ass could be so firmly muscled. Margo's throat clearing snapped my lasciviously wandering mind back to reality. I blinked a few times trying to ease the ache in my eye, and then we were off.

Remy shadowed me. His hand rested on my hip as a gentle reminder that he was right there with me. The couple of times I stopped too suddenly and he bumped into me, his fingers tightened slightly. It was flirtatious and arousing. And wrong, I knew that. As a good Samaritan, however, it was my civic duty to aid a hapless, unclothed stranger and see that he was escorted to safety. Right? Right.

Our hotel was close, thankfully, and we were able to sneak in through the rear entrance without too much fanfare, but we did manage to elicit a few wide-eyed stares from curious onlookers by the time we arrived. What was it about women gawking and checking out Remy that infuriated me and raised my defenses? The emotion I was experiencing, the possessiveness, was surprising and unfamiliar. After the slow-moving group trek and short argument about whose room we should take him to—I won—we were finally tucked safely behind closed doors.

Through the adjoining door, I was able to enter David's suite and borrow some clothes for Remy. Although, it wasn't easy to find anything due to the obvious size difference. Nodding to the bathroom, I handed Remy a few garments. "You should get dressed."

His hand clasped over mine and held a little too long. His eyes narrowed just the slightest bit again, but he nodded. I couldn't deny that as I watched him turn and walk into the bathroom, a part of me wished that I wasn't who I was and where I was.

The second the bathroom door clicked shut, Margo was on me. "Okay, spill. You slipped out to rendezvous with some serious man meat? What's going on?"

I shook my head. "No! I was outside eating my cheesecake when I heard him fall. It sounded bad. I went over and...there he was. Naked, drunk, and possibly injured."

"He doesn't look injured." Nance poked her head up from my suit-case and held up two of my blouses. "White or black?"

"White." I shook my head. "Black."

She grinned. "Scandalous."

Margo winked and clucked her tongue. "You're totally hot for him. You're all flushed and your eyes go all gaga when you look at him."

"It's nothing, Margo."

"You can't lie to me. I know you, girl. I know you well enough to know that that expression you're wearing is something new. I have never seen you have it for anyone—especially David." She threw up her hands. "And the timing. The night before your wedding. Good lord!"

The bathroom door swung opened, and a semi-dressed Remy was pouting and looking as though he'd just lost his best friend. "Your *wedding?*"

REMY

Lennox, my mate, looked shocked. She paled and her teeth dug into her plump lower lip. "Yes, tonight was the rehearsal dinner."

I fell into the nearest chair. "How?"

Despite the cautionary look her friend gave her, she stepped closer. "I just came outside to get some fresh air, and you were there..."

The room was still spinning, her words were hurling at me so quickly I was unable to grasp them all, but some must have registered because my heart was cracking. More fissures of pain and disappointment appearing by the second. "We are mates, you and me. We are meant to spend eternity with each other. Us."

Her friend held up her hands and shook her head at me. "You're a little tanked, buddy. Maybe you should wait until you sober up to declare your undying, eternal love."

"I am inebriated, true, but I am not blind or stupid. Lennox is mine." Gazing beseechingly at Lennox, I implored, "You cannot get married. Not to another."

My enhanced senses filled with the sound of her rapid heartbeat and the scent of her eagerness for me. Drunk or not, I was able to clearly detect her awareness of our bond. She must call off the wedding. Immediately.

She inched closer and placed her hand on my shoulder. We both sucked in a sharp breath at the contact.

"Wow. Okay..."

The feeling was amazing, something I'd been waiting for, but even anticipation couldn't have dreamed up the astonishing reality of it.

"We need to get you to a doctor. I think you hit your head pretty hard."

Big brown eyes. One had a spot of green along the outer edge. My yearning to study her, to learn every inch of her, to make love to her and feel her soft curves was overwhelming. Exploring her could entertain my desires for hours—days.

I blinked a few times to clear my head. Why was I smiling? I pulled my face into a frown. Whatever Armand had put in his brew this time around was too much. He was going to hear from me.

"Who's going to hear from you?"

How much had I said out loud? I looked back up at her and shrugged. "My head is fine. I had too much to drink. It sneaked up quickly, I guess."

"You guess?"

Shrugging again, my hand clasped hers. The backs of my fingers brushed her silk covered thigh. "You feel it, right?"

She looked pained, once again chewing her bottom lip, as she focused on our hands. "I..."

"*O*-kay." Her friend gently tugged Lennox away from me, ignoring my growl, and pushed her to the other side of the room. "What we're not going to do is that. What we *are* going to do is drink a few glasses of wine to see if we can catch up with Mr. Growly over there. I don't foresee the night getting any shorter."

I stood and adjusted the pants I'd been given. They were too small and too short, but they were the least of my worries. My mate was pledged to another male. She couldn't marry him. In the old world, I would've challenged him to battle, won her in a show of my savagery and skill proving myself the worthier male. That was what a male chanced by marrying someone who was not his true mate. Just as Lennox's wannabe husband was chancing by trying to claim her. He could not have her.

"We should converse. I would like to know you." Talk first, then sneak away so I could touch her.

The friend stepped in between us and shook her finger at me. For such a tiny female, she was very brave to continually step between a dragon and his mate. "You can talk to her, but I'm not going anywhere. And you'll have to talk from over there."

Lennox rolled her eyes. "Margo..."

"The two of you can say what you have to say from across the room, or we can all sit here in silence. Your choice."

I sat in the chair next to Lennox and tried to smile sweetly at the little warrior. "Good?"

She laughed. "You're lucky you're cute or this behavior of yours might warrant a call to the proper authorities."

"Margo!"

My mate did not like her friend calling me cute; I heard the challenge in her voice. Grinning, pleased by her instinct to claim me, I reassured her, "I only have eyes for you, mate."

Margo barked a laugh. "You, big guy, dial it down a notch. You look like a strutting peacock. And you! You're blushing like a schoolgirl. Stop it. You're getting married tomorrow."

I growled. "Stop saying that."

"Growl at me again and you're going to find yourself back outside."

My eyes narrowed, assessing her I wondered if she had some kind of magical powers. How she thought she was getting me out of the room was beyond me. "Are you a witch?"

"Did he just call you a bitch?"

Lennox waved the other woman away. "Calm down, Nance. He said witch."

"And if I was?"

"It would explain why you think you could separate me from my mate."

Margo shifted her gaze between me and Lennox and finally threw her hands up. "Don't get any closer."

Lennox crossed her legs, drawing my eyes like a magnet. "I...I don't know what's happening. One minute I was just eating my cheesecake and then...this."

I did not need to inquire what she meant by *this*. She was obviously feeling the magnetism between us as much as I was. The mate pull was extraordinary. It was impossible to ignore, and I had to wonder how Blaise had thought he could stay away from Chyna if she refused him. Right then and there I knew, without a doubt, that there was nothing that would keep me from Lennox. And no one.

"Maybe you should put a shirt on, Romeo?" Margo was across the room, talking to Nance in hushed whispers that I had no difficulty hearing, but stopped when she saw me leaning toward Lennox. "It wouldn't kill you."

"Of course, a shirt would not kill me. I am a dr—" Whoops! "I am a very strong male."

Lennox covered her mouth with her hand and looked up at the ceiling. "Oh, my god."

"What?" Margo and I said in unison.

"How is any of this happening? This is the night before my wedding. I'm getting married tomorrow. My wedding dress is hanging in the closet, fully paid for and altered, and the venue and the caterers and flowers and open bar and live band have all been arranged. And all has been going well, just as planned—just the way life is supposed to go. Nothing outlandish, and nothing spectacularly magnificent, you know? Because life doesn't drop spectacular and magnificent from the sky while you're trying to eat cheesecake by yourself so no one judges you about a made-up diet. No, it does not. Life gives you a mother-in-law who thinks you're fat and looks at you as though she'd eagerly rip your head off for dog chow if her poodles were hungry enough and wanted a treat!

"But here you are. All magnificent. And spectacular. And muscly. And what am I supposed to do? This must be a sign. It's clearly a sign. The man fell from the sky, for goodness' sake! Tell me that's not a sign. Oh, my god. I can't breathe."

I jumped from my chair and pulled Lennox into my arms. "You can breathe. I've got you, mate."

Margo pushed at me. "You're going to suffocate her with your big man chest!"

I held firm. "Go away, little witch. I am trying to take care of my mate."

She pushed harder. "Look at her hyperventilating! She's shaking!"

The shock of realizing Lennox's shoulders were shaking, just as her friend claimed, caused me to take a half step back. Margo gave me another shove, this one with all her weight behind it, and we all went down in a heap on the bed. I swiveled to cushion the fall for Lennox as best I could, but in my tipsy state, she still ended up half under me.

"You big oaf!" Margo smacked and shoved me. "Wait. Are you laughing, Len?"

Sure enough, Lennox was laughing, so hard that her shoulders were shaking and her face was flushed a bright red. "What's so funny?"

Catching her breath, she opened her mouth to answer when the loud knocking started up at the door. One quick sniff revealed it was a male at the door. One who had touched Lennox, but not much. He barely carried any of her scent, as much as someone who'd merely hugged her in passing might carry.

"Lennox? What's going on in there?"

Lennox froze under me. "It's David."

Margo's pointy clawed manicure dug into my arm. "You have to go," she hissed. "It's her fiancé."

"Then I am definitely not leaving."

"Don't be an asshole!"

I glared down at Margo. "She is not meant to be his. If you are a good friend, you will not push her towards a male she is not meant to be with."

"And if you are her real mate, you will not put her in a situation that will have everyone she knows gossiping and talking shit about her."

The knocking on the door intensified.

Scowling at the little witch, I finally gave in. I did not want to cause more upset for my mate. I would give her a chance to clear things up without interfering. "If he touches her, though, I'll rip him apart, limb from limb."

Chapter Six
LENNOX

Watching Remy disappear into the bathroom felt a little wrong. But that thought alone was madness. What about me made the man feel like he had more right to be in my room than my own fiancé who was supposed to become my husband in the morning?

David was who I was marrying and who I had to marry because the hotel was already booked solid with wedding guests. Because Dad had paid a pretty penny for everything. Because every detail was planned to a tee. Because it was a lavish, extravagant affair. David and my wedding had to happen.

Margo's face appeared in front of mine. "Get it together, Lenni. You want to get married to David, don't you?"

"I..." I did, didn't I? "Of course. I just... Yeah, of course. Of course, I want to marry David."

She backed toward the hotel door. "Then, maybe you should stop looking so utterly horrified."

I tried to wipe all emotion from my face as she opened the door, and David strode in with a purpose. I stood, hands at my sides, almost as though I was waiting to pass inspection. Almost-wife in her room? Check. Almost-wife still put together nicely? Not so much. Almost-wife staring at the bathroom door like it was a jumbo-sized candy bar she was attempting to sneak past her nutritionist? Double check.

"Jesus, Len, I've been knocking forever. What are y'all doing in here?"

"Just having a little fun, David." Margo smiled sweetly at him. "Shouldn't you be out painting the town on your last night of freedom?"

"You didn't come back to the table, Lenni. Everyone was worried about you." He stood in front of me and looked me over. "You look terrible. What happened to you?"

Picking at the new holes in my dress, I stuttered, "J-just got c-caught. Bushes."

Margo nodded. "Rabid bushes."

"What are you talking about?"

"I, um, tripped...and then I fell...into some shrubbery." I was wringing my hands together and toeing the ground the same way I always did when I lied. I was a terrible poker player.

Nance smiled just as sweetly as Margo. "She had a little mishap and got a few holes in that lovely dress and called us out so we could all come up here together to get her dressed in something less holey. Then, we all just figured dinner would be over, so no point in heading back. Now, like Margo said, shouldn't you be out having fun?"

"What the hell is going on here?"

His raised voice served as that last turn of the crank—the one that sprung the latch and released the jack in the box. The bathroom door flew open, and there was Remy, every towering, massive inch of him, hands on hips, wearing David's pants and nothing else. His eyes blazed as they bore into David. He even managed to look threatening in pants that were skin tight and inches too short for him.

Quick-thinking-Margo jumped in, though. "Oh, gosh, this is so embarrassing. You're not supposed to be here to see the stripper, David."

"Stripper?"

I'd never been in a situation even remotely similar and had no idea what to do. I clamped my hand over my mouth and just watched, hoping the right thing to say or do would come to me.

"Who the hell is this chump?" David looked Remy over. "And why the fuck is he wearing my pants?"

Remy growled. "Would you care for them back? They are much too puny for me, anyway."

"Who the fuck are you and why are you here?"

Margo stepped between them, waving her hands. "Okay, I told you. He's a stripper, and he's just trying to do his job, David. You're making this so awkward."

"The fuck he's a stripper. What kind of stripper puts on someone else's clothes?" He jerked his hand toward Remy. "Those were two-hundred-dollar pants, chump."

The low, menacing growl that had been rumbling from Remy's chest suddenly turned fiercer, and I was instantly aware of his mountainous physique and the slip up he'd made earlier. Referring to himself, he'd started to say something. A name that started with a d and then an r... Granted, it didn't make any sense, but then again, it was the only thing that made sense. I might not want to admit it aloud for fear of being carted off to the loony bin, but I was pretty sure that a short time ago I'd seen an enormous red creature with wings, scales, and talons. And, I was pretty sure that the creature disappeared into thin air at the same time that Remy appeared in its place. Dr...*agon*...

Dragon shapeshifter?

Right, that literally made no sense. Although...a ginormous creature one second, and a naked man the next. What other possible explanation could there be?

"I do not like you. Chump."

For some reason, Remy's simple statement made me giggle. Immediately, my hand slapped over my mouth again, and I turned away from them. "Sorry."

"You think this is funny?" David was getting riled up in a big way, and I could already hear my mother's voice lecturing me about upsetting my almost husband and my duties as his soon-to-be wife.

"You dare raise your voice to my mate?" Remy gently picked Margo up and moved her aside as though she weighed nothing more than a blade of grass. Not even a bulging muscle.

David grew red. "What the fuck is your deal? Who are you?"

"You should leave. Town."

"Fuck off. I'm getting married tomorrow, in case you were unaware. And that woman over there," if David would have pointed his finger any harder, he might have dislocated his arm, "is going to be my wife."

One wouldn't have thought it possible, but Remy grew even larger. He already towered over all of us, and he was now more imposing. "Over my dead body."

David turned away and rubbed his jaw. Then, he jerked back around and tried to sucker punch Remy in the face. Remy caught his hand and just held it. While David jerked his arm back and forth, whimpering, trying to get his hand back, Remy stood glowering at him.

"If there weren't females present, I would rip your arm off and beat you with it, you dinky little pipsqueak."

Margo smacked my arm, rousing me from my stupor. "Do something!" she hissed.

What she wanted me to do, I hadn't a clue. I stepped forward and held my hands up. "Um... Could we not do this? Please let's calm down and discuss this rationally. Without the discussion turning physical."

Remy finally let up on David's hand, and David pulled it away, cradling it to his chest. When he spoke, his voice was wobbly. "Get him out of here, Lennox. Now."

"David, he hit his head. He needs a doc—"

"Get him the fuck out, Lennox! Get him out, or you'll be standing at the altar all by yourself tomorrow!"

And there it was. My out. David had never really offered one up before. Even when he was unhappy with me, or disappointed, he just chided me and told me to work on whatever behavior he found unacceptable or lacking. He'd just spoken the magic words, though. Words that could get me out of everything. I could explain to my parents that David backed out, not me.

Getting married was something I wanted, but that was less about David and more about starting a family. PTA meetings, a dog, family movie night, meatloaf Mondays, I wanted all that. It just so happened that David had been the best offer. The only offer.

Even with my mom shoving him down my throat, and David's roving eye and nitpicking criticisms, and the fact that his mother was disapproving and, uh, difficult, we still ended up here. My dating life had been dry as a bone.

That moment was the first time in months I allowed myself to think that maybe I didn't have to marry David. That maybe there was someone else for me.

My eyes landed on Remy, and I shivered as a wave of desire shot through me and little tornados swirled in my belly. Even in front of David, I could feel it. Heady and strong, it was like a spell had bewitched me and taken over my senses.

No one moved. No one said a thing. The ball was completely in my court. I noticed Margo out of the corner of my eye, poised to take action as soon as she was needed, waiting for the signal to determine what she should do, who she should kick out.

Jumping in with both feet, I blew out a sigh and followed my gut. "David, you should go now. We need to get a doctor to examine Remy."

Chapter Seven
LENNOX

"You are kidding me." David's shocked expression clearly conveyed that he'd thought the threat of abandoning me at the altar would've straightened me out.

"No, I'm not kidding. Remy hit his head and he's been acting strange. He needs medical attention."

"Strange?" Remy and David echoed in unison.

"How do you know he's acting strange? Do you know this man?"

I winced. "A little strange."

Remy shrugged. "I have been called worse."

"Excuse me?" David looked like he was seconds from having a stroke. "What the fuck is going on? Is there something going on between the two of you? Have you been sleeping together?"

I would've had to be dead and long buried to not feel a delicious thrill of excitement at the thought of sleeping with Remy. I'd never slept with anyone, though. I'd been saving myself for my wedding night, which suddenly, in that moment's hindsight, seemed like a horrible idea. David next to Remy made my blood run cold as a terrible thought emerged. I didn't want to sleep with David. I never had the kind of desire for David that Remy inspired in me.

"Yes. She is my mate."

"Remy! No, there's nothing going on. I haven't slept with anyone. I just met him tonight."

"I don't believe you."

Margo stepped forward, shaking her head. "I was there. She's telling the truth. Not that it matters, because she asked you to leave."

"I paid for the fucking room. If I want to stay, I'll stay."

"Actually, her father paid for the fucking room." Nance stepped up beside me and wrapped her arm around my waist in a show of solidarity. "And you, of all people, David, shouldn't be lecturing or questioning anyone about who they've been sleeping with."

My face burned and I looked away. I knew about David's flirtatious nature and rumors of his little indiscretions. Apparently, so did everyone else. My mom assured me that David's behavior was normal. Dad did it. Men just did that kind of thing. It was fine. It didn't feel fine. It felt mortifying to know that the man you're supposed to marry is rumored to be banging his secretary ten ways to Sunday, all while you're sitting at home, twiddling your virgin thumbs. I had always assumed the rumors were just nasty gossip, but maybe I was incredibly naïve.

"So, what now? We just call the whole thing off because you're fucking some stripper?"

"Oh, *now* he's a stripper!" Margo threw her hands up.

"Speak to my mate like that again and I will toss you out of here." Remy stepped forward, dwarfing David.

"Fuck you, weirdo. This isn't about you. It's about my wife."

A chill traveled down my spine. I'd never heard David call me his wife before. It sounded like the steel bars of a cage being slammed shut on me. What the hell was I doing?

Remy had clearly reached his breaking point. He grabbed David by the back of his shirt and the waistband of his pants and easily hoisted him off his feet. David, hanging horizontally, four feet above the ground, screamed and thrashed. Nance rushed around the men to open the door and then, like David was nothing more than a sack of trash, Remy tossed him out into the hallway.

Nance closed the door and held up her hand for Remy to high five. "That was awesome!"

Remy stared at her hand for a second before it dawned on him what she wanted. Then he raised his hand and waved at her before turning back to me. Nance stared at his back for a second, perplexed, but quickly recovered and shrugged it off.

"So, that was a decision," Margo said gently, watching me while I attempted to steel my emotions so they didn't reveal the extent to which I was freaking out.

I cleared my throat. "Do you think so?"

"Oh, your new boyfriend just threw your fiancé out of your hotel room and you watched it happen. That was a decision being made, I am quite certain about it."

"Are you okay?" Remy passed all the invisible boundary lines Margo had drawn, but she didn't seem as readily available for crowd control anymore.

I sucked in a big breath of air that smelled like him—pine forests and dark chocolate—and felt a slight bit calmer. "I don't know. Part of me feels like my drink was drugged and I stumbled and fell down a rabbit hole."

"You think someone put something in your drink? Do you think it was that guy?"

I laughed and shook my head. He was so caring and attentive. "I just mean that everything is crazy. Nothing makes sense."

"This makes sense." He gestured between our bodies.

"This literally can't make sense."

"But it does. You are my mate. I'm yours. Forever."

I should've been running. More of that same old should've been stuff... I wasn't running, though. I was leaning into him and wondering how I'd gone my whole life without ever feeling that way before. What he was saying didn't feel insane. Somewhere deep inside, past the point of reasoning, it did make sense. I didn't understand it, but it felt right.

"I hate to break up the love fest, but your mom is calling." Margo handed me my phone and winced. "It's not going to be pretty."

I answered more out of habit than self-preservation. "Hello?"

Her angry shouts carried through the phone and echoed around the room. Loud and garbled, she was so angry that she was stumbling over her own words. The only thing that was crystal clear was that she wanted me to meet her in their room as soon as possible.

I hung up and looked around. "Crap."

Margo nodded. "Good luck."

"Maybe, I don't have to go. I could just hide out somewhere."

Nance snorted. "She'd be up here in seconds if she thought you were blowing her off."

I sat down heavily on the bed and ran my hands through my hair. "Okay. I'll go and tell her that things have changed. I'm not ready to marry David."

"Ever." Remy held out his hand. "I will go with you."

I looked at his bare chest and fanned my face. "I don't think that's a great idea."

Margo nodded. "You're drunk, half naked, and you just threw the golden boy out on his ass."

"I will not leave you to stand alone in front of your mother. I will show her that we are mates and that I am prepared to honor and care for you. She will have nothing to worry about."

I took his hand and forced a smile. "That's sweet, but I have to go alone. She's already going to be furious. If I showed up with you, I'd never get out alive."

"What?!"

I couldn't help the giggle, he was so funny. "Just a phrase. I'll be fine. Why don't you lie down and Margo will call a doctor?"

"I heal just fine on my own. I'm barely inebriated anymore."

"Just this strange naturally, then?" When he grinned at me and that dimple of his peeked out, I felt myself sway slightly, like I was the drunk one. "Okay, I'm going."

Margo stopped me at the door and took my hand. "Are you sure about this?"

"I don't know, Marg. I just know that when David called me his wife, I felt like crawling out of my own skin. Beyond that... I have no answers."

Margo shrugged and smiled sadly. "You'll figure it out. It's not like there's a time crunch or anything."

Chapter Eight

REMY

There was something in Armand's brew that wouldn't let up, and I needed to sober up faster. Chugging a bottle of water, I figured I could not stay in the room pretending that I was going to wait for some human doctor rather than heal myself.

"Where are you going?" Margo, the little witch, stood, hands on hips, scowling. "You're not going to follow her and pressure her into making this decision."

The witch would be a perfect match for Ovide. Just as stubborn and headstrong. I could picture the two of them bickering and battling the world, and each other, in all their headstrong obstinance. "I am not going to pressure anything. She is my mate. We belong together."

"I know all about this mate shit. What are you? You started to say something. Dragon? Is that what you are?"

I frowned. "How do you know about dragons?"

"Oh, come on. This is New Orleans. You think that *all* us humans are ignorant to the mumbo jumbo going on around here? Plus, my uncle mated a tiger shifter from Lafayette."

"I am not a tiger shifter from Lafayette. And it is not mumbo jumbo. It is serious."

"How do you know she's your mate?"

Was she crazy? All the enjoyment of being drunk was lost to me, replaced by crankiness and lack of coordination. "The same way I know to breathe. It's just there. My dragon knows. *I* know—from the moment I saw her, even before, when I scented her. It is why I became discombobulated and crashed into the side of a building in the middle of the city. I was not out joyriding."

"What took you so long to get here? What if she'd gone through with marrying that prick, David?"

I frowned. "I thought you wished for her to marry him?"

"Of course not. He's all wrong for her. I just want her to come to the realization on her own. It has to be *her* decision. It would have been too easy for me to encourage her to leave him for you."

I moved toward the door. "You confuse me, but I must see that she is okay."

"She's with her parents. She's fine. Besides, you can't just roam the hotel hallways looking like that."

I looked down at my bare chest and shrugged. "I'm dressed enough. She was distressed. I need to make sure that she is alright. I don't like seeing her that way."

The other friend, Nance, cleared her throat and shifted her gaze from me to Margo and back. "Dragon?"

"Don't pretend like you don't know. It was your cousin, Carly, that my uncle married."

Nance grinned suddenly and shrugged a shoulder. "You're sure about this? She's your mate, for sure? Like, *for sure*, for sure?"

I growled. "I am sure. Shifters do not get that wrong. And I must be with her."

"No. You need to rest and let Lenni make her own decision. She needs to figure this out on her own." Margo stepped toward me. "Sorry about this."

I was about to ask what she was sorry about when a burst of pain exploded at the back of my head. The room spun in front of me as I swayed, reaching out to steady myself. With nothing to latch on to, I fell forward. The floor was hard and unforgiving, but I wasn't conscious long enough for it to bother me.

. . .

Lennox

Doom and gloom followed me like a gray cloud overhead on the walk back from my parents' room. Of course, they were right. The wedding couldn't be called off now—not the night before the ceremony with the guests either at the hotel or arriving first thing in the morning. Not after Dad forked out all that money. It was irresponsible and childish to think otherwise. They had every right to be pissed at me.

David had gone straight to them to tattle. Well, not tattle. I shouldn't think that way about the man who was soon to be my life partner. The wedding would go off without another hitch. I would go through with it. David would be my husband and everything that happened tonight would just...fade away. Not matter. Once I said *I do* in the morning, that would be it.

Yet, the farther from my parents I got, the worse I felt about agreeing to go through with the wedding. I should've said no months ago when David first proposed. There was so much pressure, though, and I was terrible at saying no. The pressure to be with David had remained steady. Marrying David made sense for everyone. My parents would prosper from the business deal that would happen in the afternoon, after the wedding. Our families would be connected, and everyone would live happily ever after.

It didn't matter what I really wanted. To be fair, before meeting Remy, I hadn't been entirely sure what I wanted. I knew what I didn't want, and when faced with the choices of either David or spending my life alone, David hadn't seemed half bad. Even with the cheating rumors. Even with all the rest of his baggage. Mom had impressed upon me that being alone for the rest of my life would be a fate worse than death for someone like me, and I tended to agree. I hated the thought of never being able to have a family of my own. I supposed I envisioned my friends would settle down and start families and I would be hanging out at home alone on Friday nights with my cell in my lap waiting for someone to call me back. No one ever would. So, I'd said yes. Not to David, but to having someone to hang out with on a Friday night.

There were no take backs, apparently. I was trapped. And Mom was right—David was the best I was going to do. Remy was amazing, but he was drunk and a little strange, and possibly a dragon. Fat chance of him waking up sober and still wanting me. Not a guy like him.

Bitter, and resigned to my fate, I made my way back to my room and prayed that I didn't pass David in the hall.

Good lord, would I spend the rest of my life praying the same thing? In our home at night, when I went to grab a glass of water, would I stand with my back against the wall, peering around corners, praying that he wasn't around the next one?

It didn't matter. None of it did. I had an obligation, and I had to see it through. Marry David, follow through with my promises. It was what we Ledouxs did. We kept our word, and I wouldn't shame the family by going back on mine. Probably.

As soon as I opened the door to my room, I knew something was weird. Margo and Nance were standing right in the entryway, blocking my view of the bed.

"So, we have something to tell you."

"Something that's not a big deal. Not a big deal, at all."

I peeked around them and saw Remy half slumped over on the bed. He was unconscious, and there looked like a lump on the back of his head. "Oh, my god! What happened to him?"

"You're making it seem like a big deal."

"And it's completely not a big deal."

I glared at them and grabbed Remy around his waist. "Help me get him in the bed, you psychos. Did you do that to him? Why would you hit him?"

Margo grabbed his legs and Nance pushed as we rolled him into the bed. "He was trying to come after you. We didn't figure that would be a good idea. Not for the family meeting you were having. He heals really fast, though. Didn't you hear him say that?"

"Ugh, he weighs a ton." Nance used her legs to push and shove, and the three of us finally got him in the bed.

I cradled my face in my hands and sat down next to him. It'd taken less than two hours for my entire life to implode in front of me. And tomorrow, I was expected to walk down the aisle and act as though I wasn't marrying the wrong guy with a nut job as my maid of honor.

Chapter Nine

REMY

My head throbbed with a headache to top all headaches. "Dragons did not often have headaches..." I rolled sideways, assuming I was in my bed at home, and hit the floor. That's when I remembered it wasn't my first time crashing to the floor lately.

I sat up too fast and saw stars. Where in smoldering flames was that witch? I'd never wanted to strangle a human so much before. She'd knocked me over the head with something. Or perhaps the other one did it, the one with the tiger cousin. Either way, I had no doubt the witch was the mastermind.

Lennox wasn't in the room. No one was in the room, an observation that quickly converted my anger to gut-gnawing worry. Calling out for my mate, my shaky legs traversed the suite, investigating. The bathroom and adjoining rooms were empty. She couldn't be gone; I'd only just found her.

Heart racing with fear and dread, I jerked open the door to look out into the hallway and found the little witch standing in front of me, fist raised as though she was about to knock. "You!"

She grinned sheepishly. "Sorry 'bout last night. I couldn't let you get in the way. Turns out, you should've gotten in the way. Lennox is about to go through with it and walk down the aisle."

"What aisle?"

"The wedding aisle, you dope. I brought you clothes to change into. Hopefully, I got the size right. If you plan on saving the day, you'd better get 'em on and get moving."

"I'll just go like this."

She held up her hands. "Noooo, you will not. No girl appreciates being swept off their feet by a knight in shining armor who smells like you smell right now. Shower. Dress. Brush your teeth. Do something with your face."

"What's wrong with my face?"

"Shave it."

"That is ridiculous. You were wrong last night. You could be wrong now. I cannot let her marry him."

"I'm not wrong this time."

"Says the female who knocked me over the head. Get out of the way."

"No. The wedding hasn't started yet. You still have a little while. Get cleaned up. I'll wait out here for you. Then, I'll take you right to it. Hurry."

I swore but snatched the bag she held away from her. "If you are wrong..."

"I won't be."

I slammed the door and rushed through cleaning myself and dressing. I didn't shave my beard, but I trimmed it with the trimmers she'd included in the bag. Just a few minutes later, I was dressed in a pair of black trousers that fit well and a white button-down shirt. I rolled the sleeves up my forearms and ran a hand through my hair before throwing open the door.

Of course, Margo was absent. A note was taped to the door, and when I read it, I swore that I would strangle the witch. She'd left me. Purposely. The wedding was blocks away, in St. Matthew's Cathedral, and she thought it would be more dramatic if I burst in once the wedding was in progress. With no directions, just the name of the church, she had left me stranded.

I took off running down the hallway barefoot. I had to stop the wedding. I could not allow Lennox to marry another. No matter the reason, it was not right. She belonged to me. I was her mate. I wasn't being completely selfish. She would be miserable if she tried to make a marriage with someone else work. He was not the male for her, and it would become more and more evident. Every day, she would look at him and long to see in him the true mate that he could never be.

I took the stairs three at a time down to the main lobby and out onto the street. Questioning passersby, I learned the quickest route to St. Matthew's and took off running. My dragon desperately wanted to emerge, but I held him back. Flying would be quicker, but arriving naked would defeat the purpose of the shower and new clothes, and the witch was probably right. I should appear presentable and looking my best. Besides, revealing that I was basically a nonhuman in front of Lennox's family and guests was not a good plan, so I ran for all I was worth. Dodging people and traffic, I prayed to the gods of fire to hold off the ceremony until I arrived.

Brother, you in danger? You're putting out some stressful vibes. Blaise's voice was almost a welcome intrusion. My twin was occasionally comforting in trying moments.

I found my mate. She's getting married. I must stop it.

WOW! Do you need help?

With a groan of relief as I finally spotted the spires of the church, I dashed forward. *Maybe with murdering a little witch. My mate's friend. Perfect for Ovide.*

Part mule shifter?

I almost laughed, but my relief from arriving at the church was quickly snuffed out when I noticed that the church doors were closed. I was terrified I was too late. *I will fill you in later, bro.*

With Blaise out of my head, I crashed through the front doors, prepared to halt the proceedings and only found myself in a lobby. Another set of doors was in front of me.

My heart in my throat, this time I opened the doors slowly and stepped inside the cavernous cathedral. An organist played, the humans were standing, eyes on the female in a white gown walking down the aisle toward the front of the church. The overwhelming aroma of fresh flowers and perfumed humans did nothing to hide her scent. I stood frozen, niggling doubt working its way through me.

Would she hate me if I caused a ruckus? What if she really *did* want the wedding?

She turned abruptly.

Her flowers at her side, she drew back the white gauzy material covering her face and, when she saw me, a bright, beaming smile spread, lighting up her features. The flowers hit the floor. She started toward me—slowly at first, and then at a sprint.

My beautiful mate. I felt as though I would burst with happiness.

Lennox flew into my arms and I held her off the ground, against my chest and spun her.

"You came! I can't believe you came! I was hoping and praying you would, but I thought it was just a stupid, unrealistic fantasy on my part, but here you are."

"Of course I came. You belong with me and I came to get you." I glanced up to see several people hurrying angrily toward us.

She locked her arms around my neck and let her head fall against my shoulder. "I don't belong here, you're right. I turned around to run away and there you were."

"Good timing?"

"The best. I couldn't go through with it. I'm not sure if I would have gone through with it if I'd never met you, but I did meet you. And, David is all wrong for me."

I growled. "I am the male who will love, honor, and care for you. Not that...chump."

She peeked over my shoulder and gasped. "Let's get out of here. Fast."

Knowing that I'd be faster without Lennox trying to keep up, especially in a dress, I tightened my hold on her and bolted.

"They're following. I can't believe it. Haven't they ever seen any movie, like, ever? They're not supposed to follow!"

I ran faster, holding her tighter to my chest. No one would take her away from me. Not now, not ever. I'd like to see them try.

"Head back to the hotel, Remy."

I did as my female commanded.

Chapter Ten

LENNOX

I was in the midst of pulling the craziest caper I'd ever pulled in my life with a man I'd only met around twelve hours prior. Leaving my fiancé at the altar? Holy crap, I was a runaway bride. That was not a label I'd ever live down, surely. In that moment, as Remy carried me through the hotel and up to my room, labels, decorum, saving face, doing what was proper—none of that mattered. I'd made a decision and I'd chosen selfishly. I wanted Remy. I didn't know what it meant, but I knew that it felt right. Righter than anything I'd ever done before.

I knew people would show up looking for me. My mother would show up screaming until she was blue in the face. My father would show up and do his whole disappointed act. David would show up, spewing vile insults because I'd embarrassed him. Eleanor, his mother, would... probably send flowers. She hadn't paid for the wedding, and I knew she thought David deserved better and had "settled" for me.

I would face all that, though. Walking down the aisle toward David, I'd had a vision of what I wanted to do that night—my wedding night. Yet, it had nothing to do with David. In a moment of perfect clarity, I panicked and turned around, planning to escape back to the hotel room, hoping I'd be able, somehow, to find Remy. And there he'd been. Looking exactly like my knight in shining armor. He was perfect, and I was hoping to spend my would-have-been-wedding-night with a man that I felt a fire in my belly for.

When he carried me through the door into the hotel room, I giggled.

"Why are you laughing, mate?"

"It's silly, but I'm in a wedding dress and all, and I just had this vision of you carrying me over the threshold. That's what newly married couples do." The grin that spread over his face was ginormous. He stepped back out into the hall and carried me back over the threshold several more times grinning from ear to ear while I giggled in delight.

Finally, he put me down and stepped back to close the door. His gaze was heated as he trailed his eyes down my wedding dress and back up. "We are finally alone."

Closing the gap between us, my palms pressed up against his chest. His skin was hot to the touch, even through his shirt. "Is this as insane as I think it is?"

"It is not insane. This is how mates work."

"I don't know about mates, but I want to spend tonight with you and lose myself in this—whatever it is—that's happening between us."

"Tell me everything that you wish, mate. I will endeavor to make it happen."

I stood on my tiptoes and gently pressed a kiss to his lips. "I always wanted to wait to lose my virginity on my wedding night. I thought that it would be special that way, with a man who mattered in my life, and that it would mean everything to both of us. Like fireworks and magic. I didn't realize it wouldn't be happening with my husband, but I think the other elements are there for us, the fireworks and magic."

He gripped my waist. "I will be your husband. If that is what you wish."

I stared into his eyes and tried to determine whether he was joking. Not an ounce of humor in those golden orbs. My heart skipped. The silly little thing was pitter-pattering all over the place. It should've been alarmed by what Remy was saying, but nope, it wasn't. The man was already holding it in the palm of his hand.

"I do not want to rush you."

I turned in his arms and pressed my back into his chest. His firm erection was there already, digging into my lower back. Pulling my hair out of the way of the laces crisscrossing the back of my dress, I looked over my shoulder at him. "You would've been rushing me ten years ago. At twenty-nine and still a virgin, I'm ready."

I gasped as my dress was suddenly free. Over my shoulder, I saw his devilish grin. "What did you do?"

"You do not need this dress anymore. I took care of it."

The laces fell in shreds around my feet. He'd cut them somehow. I didn't care. It was off. That was all that mattered. Remy swiveled me to face him and pushed the bodice down to settle around my hips, leaving my chest exposed in nothing but a strapless white lace bra.

Remy's eyes glowed, just like they had when he'd looked at me the night before when I'd first seen him. He certainly seemed to like what he saw. "Beautiful."

Why it turned me on so much that he found me attractive, I didn't know. I might regret this and want to get my head checked later, but for the moment, I just jumped in and went for it.

Like he could read my mind, he stepped into my space and ran his hands down my back and into my dress, pushing it the rest of the way off my hips. He caught the backs of my thighs and pulled me up and out of the dress as I clasped my legs around his waist.

"This is insane."

"You said that." He pressed his lips to mine in a gentle kiss that curled my toes in the silk flats I still wore.

Clasping both hands around his face, I deepened the kiss, wanting more of him. The intense urge to mold myself to him had me pressing myself into him. I tilted my head and opened my lips just enough to suck his bottom lip in between mine and roll the tip of my tongue over it.

Remy growled before stroking his tongue over mine and pouring fuel onto an already blazing fire. The taste of him on my lips was nothing like I'd ever experienced. Hot and spicy, he reminded me of sweet cinnamon candy.

His hands were all over my body. Across my ass, over my thighs, up my sides. There wasn't enough room between us for him to get to my chest, but I couldn't make myself pull back. There was a magnet pulling my body into his. My hands moved over his shoulders and down his back, with the need to touch him as much as he was touching me. I ended up with my fingers tangled in his hair, locked in tight.

My tongue tangled with his, mmm, he tasted of fiery, sweet red-hot candies. Nipping at his lips and then alternately sucking them into my mouth, with each nip I got a low growl from him and I couldn't get enough of his reactions. Remy settled his hands on my ass cheeks and flexed his fingers. The effect it had on my pussy was foreign to me, but something that I wanted to learn more about. The way it separated my lower lips and exposed the sensitive inner skin to the cool air gave me goosebumps.

Kissing Remy was intoxicating. I could indulge in his kisses nonstop, but I wanted to taste more of him. When I kissed down his chin and his Adam's apple, he muttered a curse and flexed his fingers more. One of his long digits brushed the puckered skin of my ass, lightly stroking over it.

I jerked against him, shocked that he'd touched me there and more shocked that it'd felt so good. "Remy..."

His tongue tangled with mine, while his finger continued stroking me. Light and gentle, tingles shot straight to my clit. With his other hand, his fingers caressed and stroked my core. So light and teasing, so gentle and tantalizing...and frustrating.

"More." I tipped my head back and clenched my thighs around his waist. "*Please*."

His fingertip pushed into my core, and we both groaned at the sensation. "So tight."

"More, Remy. I need more." There was a wildness growing in my depths. I felt like I would die if I didn't have his hands all over me, if I didn't have him in me.

Chapter Eleven
REMY

Lennox shuddered and moaned and dug her fingers into me, pinning me to her in a silent, needy plea. I licked and tasted her skin as I carried her to the bed, holding her tightly to my chest. Kneeling on the mattress, I slowly positioned her on her back in the middle of the bed. With flushed cheeks and slightly parted lips, she watched me expectantly, and I knew I was the luckiest dragon alive.

As I leaned in to taste her delicious mouth, my hard bulge brushed against the piece of lace that barely covered her wet sex. I gasped from the fierce delight. A strong, primal pull urged me to tear off my pants and plunge my cock into her tight core, but knowing that I was the first male to take her this way stopped me. Humbled by the honor she had bestowed upon me of being her first and last lover, I vowed not to take the responsibility lightly. It was my duty and my extreme privilege to pleasure my mate.

The white lace of her undergarments was almost the same shade as her creamy skin, smooth and flushed and begging for my lips and tongue. I was captivated by the way the lace fit over the mounds of her breasts. Cupping them like a second skin. I nibbled on one of her pebbled nipples, sucking it, lace and all. Lennox inhaled sharply and gripped my shoulders. Blowing a breath over the wet lace, I smiled in delight as she moaned my name.

"Remy..."

The sound of my name on her lips as I pleasured her was one of the most satisfying things I'd ever heard. I licked and kissed and nipped down her stomach and over the lace covering her core as she squirmed and thrashed. I tasted her through the lace. I had never tasted anything as sweet and delicious as my mate's juices of arousal. I quickly tore the lace off her and spread her thighs with my hands. Leaning in as close as possible, I delved into her folds, unable to get enough of her, tasting and licking her sweet sex.

Guided by her mews and whimpers, I explored and committed to memory which touches sent her body shivering, which caresses made her squirm, and which strokes of my tongue made her cry aloud.

Greedily lapping her sweet, salty flavor, I held her still and took my time devouring the prize she'd given me.

"Remy! I need more. I need to come." Lennox twisted and writhed under me, her nails raking across my scalp.

I sat back and stared down at her, bare and open to me, and was filled with awe. My female. Perfect. Exquisite.

Impatient. She sat up and unhooked her breast undergarment, threw it across the room, and with a wild look on her face, she came at me. Buttons flew off my shirt as she ripped it open.

"You've been teasing me." She pushed me backward and fumbled at the closure of my pants. "I need you, Remy. I've waited for twenty-nine years to lose my virginity and you're taking your sweet time. I'm ready. Now."

I laughed through my nose as I raised my hips for her to slide my pants down, letting her rapidly undress me. "Did you not enjoy my licking your sex?"

She stopped and raised an eyebrow at me. "Not the point."

I laughed aloud, pushed her back on the bed and hovered over her. "It *is* the point." I grinned wickedly. "I promise that you will not be leaving this room with your virginity, my mate. I will taste every bit of you, though. Your body is a feast to be savored and enjoyed. Every curve, every delicious inch."

Biting her lip, she raised her hips, her thighs quivering. "I feel like I'm going to burst, Remy. I've never felt so empty and wanting."

I rested on my side beside her and trailed my fingers down until I was cupping her sex. "I will help."

She gripped my arm, digging her nails in as I pushed my finger into her tight channel. When I pushed another in, she rolled her head back and pressed it into the pillow, the muscles in her neck stretched taut.

I rolled my thumb over the sensitive little nub at the top of her sex, while she greedily grasped at my fingers that were sliding in and out, slick and wet with her desire. I rolled slightly so I could reach her better, and when my smallest fingertip lightly pressed against her bottom, her nails scored my arm and she sat up.

The confusion showed on her face along with the pleasure as the new angle pushed my fingers in deeper. I teased my fingertip farther into her bottom and rolled my thumb faster. Pleasure warred with the new sensation at her back end, and she gripped my arm hard, her eyes boring into mine, her body quivering with every stroke.

"It is okay, mate. Let go."

As though I'd spoken magic words giving her permission, Lennox's whimpers turned to cries, which turned to screams when I slid a third finger into the wet heat of her core and curled them. Her hips bucked and her core flooded and pulsed around my fingers, tight bottom pulling my little finger in deeper. I continued to pleasure her, feeling her sweet release as she clenched and squeezed around my fingers.

Watching my mate come apart, smelling her delicious aroma, hearing her cries of pleasure, I lost the control I'd been holding onto so well. I rolled her onto her stomach and then grasping her thighs, pulled her to her hands and knees and positioned my weight over her.

With her pussy hot and wet and her thighs slick with her release, I nuzzled her neck and peppered kisses on her cheek and temple, my cock resting against her folds. When she looked back over her shoulder at me, her eyes were filled with need and lust and dazed arousal. I nearly embarrassed myself and spilled my seed on her thigh.

I had never before experienced a pleasure quite like the way I felt seeing her rapturous need for me. I eased the tip of my cock in, and although she was dripping wet, she was still very small and tight.

Cautiously, I pressed harder, and when I detected a faint scent of blood, I froze.

Her eyes were wide, but when I started to pull out, she reached behind her and grasped my thigh, urging me on. After a second or two, as I pushed into her another inch, her moan was one of pleasure, which became one of imploring and urging for more as I slid all the way in until the backs of her legs hit the front of mine.

Lennox wiggled her bottom and threw her head back. I leaned over her and cupped her chin so she'd look back at me. While she held my gaze, I pulled out and then thrust back in.

"Remy! Yes!" She dropped her head when I let her go but, again, she pushed her ass back into me. "*More.* Don't stop."

I could not have stopped if I wanted to. I pulled back and then thrust into her again. Her shivers and cries driving me, I gripped her hips and did it again. Another slow exit and a smooth, long slide back into her hot body. I could feel the pressure building between us, a demand for something more. The next time I thrust into her, it was faster, harder. Lennox's answering scream of pleasure was all I needed to know.

I'd meant to make sweet love to my mate, but the dragon demanded more. The minx under me demanded more.

Fucking her harder, I gripped her shoulders to keep her steady and lost myself in the pleasure until I felt her reaching a climax again. Her screams had all blended into one long wail of pleasure. I pumped in and out of her faster, hard. The sound of our flesh meeting again and again filled the room, mixing with my grunts and her cries. I was holding on by a thread.

I wanted to orgasm with her this time. I moved my hand back to her ass and squeezed it once before sliding my finger down to that sensitive spot she seemed to respond so well to. Pressing my finger into it, I felt her muscles push back, and then my fingertip slipped in.

Lennox's arms slipped out from under her and she let her cheek rest on the bed while her fingers dug into the blankets. I slipped my other hand under her and found her little button. Rubbing her there and thrusting into both of her holes, I felt the fires of release boiling in me.

"Come with me, Lennox." I pumped into her with shorter strokes, the beginning of my orgasm starting. "I'm going to release my seed in you, mate. I want to fill you."

Lennox's body tightened, her core gripped my cock in an iron fist, her cries grew louder and more intense, and with a shudder, her sweet release flooded her channel. The perfume of her arousal was everywhere in the room, speaking to me in the most base, primal, overwhelming way. My cock throbbed and my seed shot from me, filling her in spurts as I'd promised. A wild roar ripped from my throat as I completely possessed my mate. Her body kept contracting in pulses, lengthening my orgasm until she had milked me dry.

All of my energy zapped for the moment, I rested my body on top of hers, both of us shaking from what we'd just experienced. I'd never felt any pleasure comparable. My mate was perfection. I knew I would never get enough because, even as fought to catch my breath and my seed leaked out of her, I wanted her again.

Chapter Twelve

LENNOX

"I'm a high school teacher."

"High school. They are difficult at that age, no?"

Smiling, I leaned up on my elbow so I could watch Remy as we talked. "You sound like you know from experience."

"I do not. But I am acquainted with someone who is raising her nephews that are in high school. They have had—incidents."

Why did Remy mentioning another woman turn my brown eyes green with envy? Acquaintance *shm*aintance, I didn't care if she was an eighty-year-old great-granny, I didn't want to hear about another woman. But I reined in my irrationality. The last thing I wanted to do was argue on the best night of my life. "Um, some of them are tough. Some of them are great, though. They're smart and eager to take in as much information as they can."

He grunted. "Nick and Casey are smart. Especially when it comes to video games. My friend, Beast, has helped them become more disciplined, too, and their behavior has improved."

"You have a friend named *Beast?*"

He nodded and trailed his finger down my side. I could feel his erection growing again against my thigh. We'd had sex so many times already that I was sore. I didn't want to, but I had to take a break. My body wasn't used to the erotic gymnastics that sex with Remy was.

"I do not want to talk about other males."

So, he was feeling as possessive as I was. I liked that. Grinning, I ran a finger over his frown. "You brought him up."

"I regret it."

"What do you do?"

Remy's frown deepened, and he averted his gaze. "It is complicated."

"Try me."

"I am not really from around here." When he met my eyes, he seemed to be watching my response carefully. "Where I am from, my brother and I were leaders in our...area."

"Leaders...like CEOs or elected officials or law enforcement, what?"

"I don't think so."

I frowned. "Like what, then?"

"I do not want to say. I don't want you to think less of me. I only want to make you proud. I am not that person anymore, so it does not matter."

I wrapped my arm over his waist and hugged him tightly. He was right. It didn't matter who he'd been, but whatever it was in me that had convinced me that he was the man for me was also damned sure that he was a good guy. "Right. We can talk about it later. I won't judge, Remy."

"My people... We are very different. I have much to tell you." He paused. "I am hesitant."

His admission elicited a grin from me. "What are you afraid of?"

"My brother and friends are like me, but their mates are like you. When their mates found out about them...some found it difficult to accept. I do not want you to push me away."

I was pretty sure he was a fierce badass dragon, yet he was speaking with such vulnerability. It was doing things to my heart. I held out my pinky. "I promise that I won't judge you over what you tell me."

He stared at my pinky. "What's that?"

Laughing, I took his little finger and linked mine to his. "It's a pinky promise. A little immature, but I'm around more teenagers than adults, so it's all I've got. It's a symbolic way of solidifying a promise."

Sitting up, his pinky held mine tightly, and his gaze turned serious. "I pinky promise that I will care for you always, mate. I will never leave your side."

Again, I should've been weirded out. True, undying love didn't happen overnight. I watched my teenagers think they were in love with someone new every other week. I knew love didn't bloom instantly, but what I knew and what I *felt*... As soon as I saw Remy, I'd felt like I knew him. Something in me had recognized him, and that something had no doubts. Maybe my soul had been waiting on him for so long it had almost given up. But he'd magically appeared, right out of the sky, just in the nick of time.

"Is this magic?" My eyes blinked to clear away the emotional tears forming in the corners. "It feels like something magical. Enchanted."

We sat facing one another, my legs over his, our stomachs almost touching. "Ancient magic. Mate, long before either of us were born, we were designed for each other. Designed and created to seek out one another. My people hold mates in the highest regard. A mate is the best thing that will ever happen to a male and this is the best day of my existence.

Wow, okay, was I suddenly in one of those old-time Disney animations with fluttery butterflies and chirpy bluebirds and little forest animals dancing around? Sure felt that way—like I was a princess in a fairy tale.

"I'm sorry I almost messed up and married David."

He growled. "I would have killed him."

I just raised my eyebrows.

"You. Are. Mine."

Nope, that didn't even scare me. Because he was right. I *was* his. "I was backing out of the wedding even before I saw you, you know. I couldn't go through with it."

"I know."

"I don't pretend to understand this thing between us. Not really. I hear what you're saying, but it's all very foreign to me. Still, it didn't take me long to recognize that this was what I'd been waiting for. I didn't love David. I don't think I even liked him very much. I just got caught up in all the hoopla and... I was afraid that no one else would marry me."

"Any male would be lucky to marry you. I would marry you right now."

I grinned. "I snore."

"And?"

"Not just light snoring. I snore like a grizzly. So loud you might never get a good night's sleep again."

He simply shrugged. "I don't care. It will be worth it."

"What if I have other bad habits? Like not putting the top back on the toothpaste?"

"Is that something you are supposed to do?"

I hissed. "*Yeah*. Put the lid back on the toothpaste."

"Fine."

"Only a barbarian wouldn't put the lid back on," I teased.

He looked away. "Yeah."

Catching his face between my hands, I made him look at me. "I saw you—"

A loud pounding at the door startled me silent. Instantly, I had an urge to dive under the covers and bury myself—hide. Whoever it was, they were an intrusion and I didn't want to face a soul.

My cell started ringing on the end table. Between the pounding and the ringing, the sudden chaos shot my anxiety level skyrocketing. It had been so great, Remy and me all alone on our very own "hotel room island" before the world started closing in on us.

"You are trembling, Lennox." Remy growled at the door and easily slipped out of bed, leaving me in it and pulling the blanket over my naked body. "I will tell them to go away."

Afraid of who was at the door, I pulled the blanket over my head and tried to be as still as possible. I hated confrontation. I just wanted to wimp out.

Muffled sounds penetrated the blanket: Remy yanking open the door, a startled gasp from the other side, a low, ominous growl...

"Where's my wife, asshole?" David's words were slurred. Besides being an unwelcome intrusion, he was clearly three sheets to the wind.

A few seconds after the door closed, the bed dipped beside me. Remy pulled the cover away from my face, smiling down at me. "It was no one important. We should play some music, just in case 'no one' comes back. I believe I might almost feel bad about punching 'no one.' He has just lost the best thing that he will ever have."

I grabbed for the remote on the bedside table while also reaching for Remy. "You're sweet."

"Hardly."

I poked buttons until music started playing. "I think you *are* sweet."

"Did you forget what I have been doing to you? Was that *sweet?*" He said it like being called sweet was an insult. "Maybe I need to refresh your memory."

Refresh away. Who was I to stop him?

Chapter Thirteen

LENNOX

"I must feed you," Remy spoke from the chair next to the bed where he sat watching me. In only black trousers, he was leaning back with his hands folded across his stomach. I vaguely thought about reaching for my phone so I could capture the moment and snap a pic of him like that. Then I could sneak glances at it while I was in the middle of teaching geometry proofs. Like a midday pick me up.

"I am hungry, now that you mention it."

The minibar snacks we'd been devouring weren't enough to sustain us. Not with the energy we were burning. I reached for the packet of peanuts. Crumbs.

"You finished the peanuts."

He shook his head. "That was you."

Oh, yeah, it had been. Sleeping with Remy had me a little disoriented. I wasn't even sure what time it was, or if it was still my ex-wedding day. It might still be daytime, but the hotel drapes were thick and closed. I stood and walked to the windows.

"Blazing scales, you're stunning."

Flashing a grin over my shoulder, I pulled the curtains open a crack —just enough to see out. Twinkling city lights peppered the blanket of twilight. As I wrapped my arms around myself, watching the headlights of cars passing under us, I felt a heaviness on my chest that had something to do with coming back down to the real world and what I had yet to face.

"What were your parents like, Remy?" When he didn't answer, I turned away from the window and found him standing a few feet behind me, his warm, golden eyes suddenly cooler. "Forget I asked." Reaching out to touch his chest, I shrugged the question off.

He caught my arm and pulled me into him. "No, it's okay. It has been a long time since they passed. It is still a sore topic, I suppose."

"I'm sorry."

"You did not do it." He pressed a kiss to the top of my head. "We need food. I do not want to leave you here alone. Will you go with me?"

Feeling the heaviness on my chest press down harder, I turned back to the window. "I'll be fine here, Remy. Honest."

Hugging me from behind, he rested his chin atop my head. "What is wrong, mate? I can feel your melancholy like a dagger to my heart. Did I not please you?"

I laughed. "Is that a legit question?"

He shrugged.

I turned to look up at him. "It's not you. It's my parents. They're horrid sometimes. That's probably not the nicest thing to say around a person who's lost his parents, but mine are...awful. My mother is pushy, and she knows that if she nags me enough, she'll get her way. I don't like fighting with her, so I just cave.

She pushed me into dating David and then into the engagement. I should've said no at some point. I just went along with it all. Even when I had second thoughts and mentioned slowing things down, she was livid. She wanted to tie our family to David's. Now, she's going to be a living nightmare."

"We will face her together."

I shook my head. "That would just make it worse. And I don't want you to see me get ripped apart by my mother. It's embarrassing that I'm almost thirty and she still treats me like I'm a child. My dad's no better. He just nods along in agreement to whatever she says. The only time he ever speaks up is when she's on a rant and asks him to agree.

He doesn't care about me or what happens, as long as I don't make Mom angry enough that he has to deal with her.

It's pretty messed up, I guess. I almost married a man who I would have been miserable with because she insisted on it. I should be livid, too. I should be so angry that I throw a temper tantrum right back at her. Instead, I just feel sad. I don't want to fight. I hate fighting." I blew out a big gust of breath. "I just wish she was a normal mother who would support me and love me for who I am. That would be awesome."

Wearing a pained look, Remy ran his hand through his hair and then pulled me back into his body, hugging me tight again. "It is difficult for me to witness your pain without doing something to fix it. Tell me what I can do."

I smiled into his chest. "Feed me. Maybe I'm just hangry."

"*Hangry?*"

"Hungry-angry."

"Is that something that happens to you?"

"You have no idea."

Remy hesitated and then stooped lower to be eye to eye with me. "My mother was an angel to my brother and me. She did everything that was asked of her and never fought back when my father was a demon to her. I loved her, but I wish she would have left us. It would have been the only way to fight him, to leave, and she deserved her own happiness. You deserve your own happiness, too. Sometimes, you must run—or fight. Whatever you feel is necessary to do regarding your parents, I will be beside you."

I blinked rapidly, but it did nothing to stop tears from falling. An overwhelming abundance of emotion bubbled up from his words and from the support he offered. It didn't make any sense, the tether binding my heart, mind, and emotions to this man whom I just met. I'd dated David for over two years, and I'd never felt anything like this. With Remy, after a little over twenty-four hours, I was already thinking that this must be what that four-letter word I'd never said to a man before felt like.

"Is this more hanger?"

I laughed and hiccupped. "Yeah, maybe."

"Come on. Get dressed. We are going to go out for dinner."

"What if we run into my parents in the hotel lobby? Or worse, David's parents?" I felt my face going red. "Or any of the many hotel guests that were supposed to be at my wedding this morning? Oh, god. I really did that this morning. I ran away from my own wedding and left David at the altar in front of just about everyone I know."

"Technically, I carried you away."

I gave him a wide-eyed look. "What do I do if we run into someone? They're going to treat me like I'm some horrible, nasty person. Everyone loves David."

"If so, I will eat them."

"Remy, I'm serious."

"I am, too."

Chapter Fourteen
REMY

I studied Lennox as the elevator ascended to the third floor, where her room was located. She was staring at the doors, a look of worry clouding her face. She'd been anxious the entire time we dined. Terrified to run into someone she knew, I suspected. I couldn't say I completely understood, but I had not been kidding when I'd told her that I would eat anyone who upset her. She was such a kind and gentle female. I would protect her at any cost.

My mate. I smiled when she tugged her bottom lip between her teeth and squeezed my hand. She was stronger than she looked if her grip was any indication. "It is okay, mate."

She looked up at me and offered a tight smile, then back at the door, like she was afraid it was going to open and catch her off guard. "I have a feeling..."

"What is it?"

"I just feel like my parents are going to be up there, waiting." She sighed heavily and pushed her shoulders back. "There's no way they're gonna let this go. And when I am forced to face them, it isn't going to be pretty."

Like she'd spoken the words into existence, the doors slid open and she stiffened, emitting a little gasp. Her beautiful face paled, and her fingers tightened like a vice grip on my hand.

"Mom. Dad."

The couple in front of us looked like normal humans except for the expressions on their faces. Those were the faces of potential murderers. Responding to the hostility on the older female's face, I stepped in front of Lennox and growled a warning. She would not threaten my mate, mother or not.

"Lennox Danielle Ledoux. I need to speak to you in your room, pronto." The woman hissed the words out, her teeth bared as she glared around me. "Your, *ahem*, escort, can leave now. He's done quite enough damage."

"I will not leave."

Lennox's fingernails were cutting into my palm. Instead of saying anything to the harsh female, she just stepped out of the elevator, doing everything she could to make herself appear smaller. With slumped shoulders, she led the group of us down to her hotel room. Her hands trembled as she slid the keycard into the slot and opened the door.

I stepped into the room after her and quickly closed the door before her parents could come in. "Say you don't want them in here and I will keep them out, Lennox. It is your choice."

Her eyes grew wider, her shock quickly turning to horror. "It's going to be worse. Just...just let them in and it'll be over soon."

I pulled her into a tight hug and kissed her. "Alright, but remember, say the word..."

"And you'll eat them?"

I gave her a predatory grin. "Try me."

"Okay, let them in. It'll be okay." She crossed to the bed and sat on the edge of it, looking like a youngling preparing for a scolding.

That look sent a pang that felt like an arrow through my heart. It brought back memories of the way my mother looked sitting, waiting for my father to come and dole out the punishment he deemed appropriate for whatever imagined slight she'd committed. The thought triggered a white-hot rage in my veins, and I had to pause with my hand on the doorknob for a second in order to get my dragon under control.

With a deep breath, I pulled the door open and was met by twin glares of fury. I was pleased that their fury was focused on me. I could certainly bear it. As soon as they turned to their daughter, I would have difficulty restraining myself from ripping out their throats.

"What the hell is wrong with you?"

Lennox stood up, a polite smile on her face. You'd almost never know that the room was filled with so much tension. "Mom, Dad, this is Remy. Remy, this is my mom and dad, Lisa and Doug."

"Do not introduce us. I don't care who he is, or what rock he crawled out from under. You, young lady, have done so much damage. Do you even know the trouble you've caused? You've disappointed us before, but this goes far beyond anything you've pulled in the past. What in the world possessed you to run out of the cathedral this morning?" Lisa, the mother, glared and waved her hands in the air, emphasizing her ire. "Obviously, you were out of your mind to run away from a prestigious marriage like that. Most young ladies would kill to have a husband like David. Do you know how long we've been trying to get into business with the Thibodeaux family? Do you?

"They've already walked away from the deal. Two million dollars, down the drain like it was water. And you with barely a penny to your name. A teacher. You'll never see two million in your entire career. How dare you pull a stunt like that!

"Not to mention you leaving in the arms of another man—like some common street whore!"

I jerked the door open so hard the top part of it came off the hinges. "Get out!"

Lennox steepled her fingers over her mouth, her eyes so wide they looked like they might fall out of her head. "Remy..."

"You want two million dollars for your daughter? I will give you two million if you get the blazing scales out of here and keep walking. I thought humans stopped the practice of selling their daughters like cattle years ago." I gestured angrily toward the open door, fighting the urge to pick them both up and toss them into the hallway.

Lennox's mother glared right back at me. The backbone of the woman would have been impressive if she wasn't using it to repeatedly stab her daughter. "Like you have two million. Look at you. You don't even have shoes. And what you did this morning..."

"Rescued a kind, generous female from being forced into marriage with a man who is far beneath her? A marriage that would have slowly destroyed her?"

"That marriage was important!"

"I'm sorry, Mom. I just couldn't do it." Lennox was biting her lip so hard she was going to draw blood.

"Of course, you couldn't. You couldn't help your family, could you? Ungrateful brat. This is the last straw, Lennox. This is it. You've pushed us too far. Do you know how much money your father wasted on that wedding? And this room? The room you used like a cheap hussy to hook up with a lowlife stranger."

I lost it. Roaring loud enough to shake the room, I felt the change happening, my skin tingling, my body stretching out. I fought it back, not an easy feat, and then let out an angry puff of fire. It wasn't the most desirable way to reveal my dragon to Lennox, nor the wisest, but I was barely hanging on.

"I am seconds from turning into the biggest monster you've ever seen and making all your worst nightmares come true. If you value your measly existence, you will hold your tongues.

Lennox and I are leaving. We are going to go somewhere private, where we can enjoy each other without insults and accusations. You will go back to your miserable lives and be grateful you have such a caring, loving, forgiving daughter that neither of you deserves. She is, after all, the only reason I have not already plucked your heads from your bodies."

I held my hand out to Lennox and let out a silent breath of relief when she came. She was not afraid of me. I had been fearing I might have to scoop her up and take her out kicking and screaming. I did not bother looking back as we headed to the elevators.

Chapter Fifteen
LENNOX

The elevator climbed to the top floor of the hotel. We got out and Remy led me to the stairway where we ascended even higher. Why wasn't I freaked out by what had just happened? Remy had threatened to eat my parents and had even spit a little fireball at them. That was cool. He'd ripped the hotel door clean off its hinges. Yet, as we reached the rooftop, fear of Remy was the farthest thing on my emotional radar. I was exhilarated. And flattered. No one had ever defended me the way he had before.

We stepped out onto the roof of the hotel, and Remy turned to look at me, a worried expression pulling his features taut.

"I am going to show you something, and I do not want you to be frightened, Lennox, but this may be alarming." Remy was bent forward, staring into my eyes as he spoke. He thought I was going to blow a gasket.

"I've already seen, remember? Through the bushes when you fell. Just do it."

He looked shocked, but his eagerness for us to leave the hotel powered through. "Back up."

I stepped back and watched as he disappeared, and in his place stood a large, crimson dragon. I stood with my mouth agape. Seeing him behind some bushes and seeing him up close were two very different things. He was huge. Magnificent. I wanted to explore him, but even by New Orleans standards, a giant dragon on a rooftop was strange.

He motioned to his back and I hurried forward. Enthusiastically, I climbed onto his back and settled with my thighs wrapped around his wide neck, not unlike mounting a horse. Leaning forward to hug him, I let out a wild scream as air rushed over me and we shot into the night sky.

New Orleans was instantly twinkling lights below us, and the heavens twinkling stars above us. I laughed wildly and sat back. "Remy! This is amazing!"

Hold on. The command floored me.

"Did you just speak to me, *in my head?*"

Hold on, mate. I would not like to have to catch you in midair as you fall to earth.

I wrapped my arms tightly around him, stroking the mighty scales that coated him. I didn't know what it said about me, but my body was going crazy. Whether it was the new side of Remy, the height, the adrenaline, I didn't know. I just knew I wanted him to land and go back to his human self so we could have another round of screw-me-into-oblivion sex.

You want me to screw you into oblivion, huh? What a naughty transformation my mate has undergone in just a day. I like it.

"You can hear my thoughts?"

The ones you are screaming at me.

"Whoa! This is wild." I shouted aloud as he dipped lower and then shot back up higher. The wind whipped my hair into a wild rats' nest, but I didn't care. I really was like a Disney princess. I was riding through the night sky on the back of a dragon—and I never wanted it to end.

You are not afraid?

How could I be afraid of him? I pressed a kiss to his neck and heard him growl in response. "Take us down and I'll show you how unafraid I am."

Hold tight.

Suddenly, we were dropping fast. He flew between trees and close to a marshy body of water, splashing me, and then landed on what looked like a small dock in the middle of the bayou. Before I could adjust myself and swing my leg over to dismount, he was already shifting back and grabbing me.

He looked down into my eyes with a stunning golden stare, and I watched the golden veins and red patchy scales glitter over his skin before fading. He held my face in his hands and growled. "Flying has never felt like that. I feel like I could conquer an entire army alone." He kissed me hard and then lifted me into his arms. "I only have one thing I want to do right now, though."

I let my head fall back and stared up at the stars. It was so dark that they looked like twinkling gems I could reach up and pluck. A view that must be normal to Remy, who could fly so high. I met his heated gaze. "I'm never using my legs again. Just fly me from place to place, dragon."

He laughed. "Ah, she has become the bossy high school teacher, now?"

I cupped his face and stroked my thumb over his lips. "No one has ever fought for me like you did. You stood up to them."

"I don't think you understand, yet, Lennox. I would literally turn into my dragon and eat whole anyone who hurts or upsets you. You are my mate, and I will defend you to my death. No one talks to you like that. The only reason they are still standing is that they are your parents."

I shivered.

"Does that frighten you?"

I didn't want to say what I was thinking out loud, afraid that it made me the real monster. Instead, I closed my eyes and rested my forehead against his.

"You don't have to say anything, mate. I know you do not want anything to happen to them."

"It just feels so good to have someone in my corner. I don't know how to fight them. I know I should stand up to them and fight for myself, and maybe someday I will. But right now, I feel amazing. Better than amazing. I feel so *free*." I threw my hands in the air and twirled in a circle.

"You are free, Lennox. You can choose whatever you wish." He moved away from me and held his arms out. "Tell me where you want to go, what you want to do. I will make it happen."

I reached down and slowly pulled the hem of my shirt over my head. Tossing it aside, I met his gaze and smiled as I unbuttoned my pants. "Right now, I want you."

"I will make that happen."

Chapter Sixteen

LENNOX

I sat on Remy's patio, nearly two weeks later, staring out over the water and wondering how I was going to break it to him that I had to leave. I meant to tell him that my vacation time would soon be over, but I'd been so caught up milking every second of the best vacation of my life. I didn't want to throw a damper on it by mentioning its end. Day after day of pleasure and happiness tended to turn my brain to mush, I guessed.

I'd let everything go. I hadn't talked to anyone besides Remy, not even Nance or Margo. I hadn't been out of his house, other than to sit on the patio where we watched fireflies, listened to bullfrogs, and swatted mosquitoes. We couldn't keep our hands off each other. I'd barely worn clothes for two whole weeks, and I had an impressive lack of tan lines to show for it. In the back of my head, however, the fact that this was all make-believe had grown larger and larger. Well, it wasn't all make-believe. Remy and I were real. But walking around naked without a care in the world was coming to an end. I was going to have to deal with real life starting tomorrow.

I felt a little guilty for shutting everyone out. Margo and Nance might be worried for all I knew. No one knew exactly where I was or how to locate me. I'd meant to call, but as one day turned to another, I just didn't. It was easy to get lost in Remy. The honeymoon was ending, though.

Remy was not going to be happy about me leaving. I was upset, too. It wasn't easy to leave paradise, but lesson plans and staff meetings beckoned.

I was head over heels for Remy already. Hell, one night with him was all that took. Being with him was so easy. Talking to him and opening up to someone who actually cared was so refreshing and comforting. I loved every minute of it. I loved *him*.

Sighing, I brought my knees up to my chest. I *did* love him. Probably from the moment I'd seen him. It was intense and demanding, something so deep that I felt it in every fiber of my being.

I had to go back to my life, though. The question that plagued me —that had my stomach in knots—was whether he'd want to come along. Or at least show up some of the time. I didn't know how it worked, the whole mate thing. He hadn't told me he loved me. We hadn't talked at all about moving in or being together in the real world —the one where I lived.

I knew he cared about me. I could hear him thinking about me sometimes. He cared a lot. But that was while we vacationed in paradise. How would all those feelings transfer to late nights on the job, bills, frantic morning commutes, and the regular stresses of life? I worked full time and then some. I was always tutoring kids after school, or before, or spending late nights grading papers and planning lessons. Outside of that, I hung out with Margo and Nance, and I had family dinners once a week at my parents' house. Although...maybe we could nix the dinners.

David had fit into my life easily because we didn't really want to see each other too often. But Remy? He would demand my time, and I would want to give it.

I'd been arguing with myself over and over. Part of me, the part of me that was so stupidly, naively in love with Remy that she couldn't think straight when he was around, wanted to just walk away and leave it all behind. But I'd worked hard to carve out my niche in life. I'd faced negativity from my parents nonstop and still managed to follow through with my teaching degree. I couldn't throw away the one thing that I'd managed to make my own.

Remy was easy to talk to, but I hated to upset him. I also didn't want to have to wake him up the next morning and ask for a flight home at the same time as I told him that I was leaving.

I sat there for another hour before Remy joined me. He scooped me up, sat down on the lounger, and settled me on his lap. Wrapping his arms around me and holding me, he nuzzled his face into my neck.

"I slept too long."

I stroked his arm and swallowed a lump. My big dragon man. I didn't want to go, but mostly I didn't want things to change. I was terrified it would fall apart.

"What is wrong, my mate? You are trembling." He turned me around so I was straddling him and pushed my hair out of my face. "What has upset you?"

I didn't want to say it.

"Lennox?"

"I have to leave!" I blurted it out and then slapped my hands over my face. I buried my face in his chest and let the tears leak out.

"What are you talking about?"

Through sobs, I tried to tell him. "Work. I have to go back to work. Tomorrow. I work and then I tutor and I'm not going to have time to lounge around naked and I'm so sorry. I don't want to go, but I have to. And I have to call Margo and Nance and even my parents. I'm sorry."

Remy held me as I shook and wiped tears away. When I'd finally calmed down some, he pulled my face to his and gently kissed me. "We can leave tonight."

Jerking up, I blinked a few times to give myself time to process what he was saying. "You're coming?"

"Did you think I would let you leave without me?"

"I didn't know..."

"We are mates. I told you about mates." He had told me about how when a dragon finds a mate, it's for life. That he marks her with a bite somewhere visible like the neck. He assured me that it wouldn't be painful, but it would scar. This informs all other dragons that she's taken. He trailed his fingers over the tender skin on my neck—the skin that he still hadn't marked. He told me we were mates, but as for that bite…maybe he was waiting for a special moment or something. "Where you go, I go."

That was a huge relief. My heart smiled at how accommodating and eager to please me he was, but I felt even guiltier for not saying anything before. "I'm sorry I didn't tell you sooner."

"Lennox, why are you apologizing to me?"

I felt my cheeks burn. "I just…I should've told you."

He rubbed his thumbs over my cheeks and shrugged. "You told me now."

"Wait a second…" I sat up straighter and narrowed my eyes at him. "You knew, didn't you?"

With a sly grin, he averted his eyes. "I figured you'd tell me when you were ready. For the record, mate, you scream most of your thoughts at me."

Smacking his chest, I climbed off him and slid to the next chair. "Here I was so worried!"

"There is nothing to worry about. I am yours. You need only to relay your thoughts and feelings to me. We will figure everything out together. Okay?" He looked down at his lap and back at me. "Now. If you're done being upset, I'd like my mate back on my lap."

I tried to hide my giggle, but it was pointless with him. "Can you hear my thoughts right now?" I rested my hands on his chest and trailed my fingertip over the line of an old scar.

"You are wondering if things will be the same once we return to New Orleans. And the answer is yes, I believe so. We will be together. That's what matters."

"Will you be okay there?" I looked around at his property. It was basically a mansion—he called it a castle—tucked deep within secluded swampland. "I live in an apartment. There's not even a great view."

"It will be okay. We will make it work."

I hoped so.

Chapter Seventeen

REMY

How is mated life, bro? I haven't heard from you in weeks. You must bring your mate over soon. Chyna, Cherry, and Sky are asking constantly to meet her. Seems they have noticed some similarities between the three of them and are wondering if the similarities extend to Lennox.

I rolled my neck and went back to searching Lennox's minuscule bathroom for those pills she eats when she has a headache. I had already torn apart the kitchen pantry where she kept a few medicines. Why they were all spread out, I didn't know. I did not even know if her human medicines would work for me.

All I knew was the myriad of sounds and the hundreds of smells surrounding me were driving me slowly insane. They were not sounds of the natural environment I was used to—the wildlife in the swamps, marshes, and wetlands. There was also human stink. Not Lennox's scent. Hers I loved. It was from the others in the building, some of it natural, much of it artificial—an overabundance of perfumes, deodorants, hair products, detergents. It was enough to drive a dragon insane.

The stomping from upstairs started up again and I growled. I would soon go up there and break someone's legs.

Mated life was not exactly what I thought it was going to be. I had been staying at Lennox's apartment for a week, and already I was pacing the place angry and irritated. I was more than bored, I felt as though I was in a cage that was too small and had a constant barrage of human voices. With my enhanced hearing, I could hear everyone in the building, laughing, talking, arguing, snoring, fucking, everything. Constantly.

Mated life is great.

Remy, what is wrong?

I slammed the cabinet door closed, cracking it. That was another thing. I kept breaking things. It was as though the apartment was made of cardboard and bubblegum. Every time I touched something, it broke or fell apart. Examining the crack, I thought of what Lennox would say when she saw it. She would not be happy. She would sigh as though she had lost patience with a youngling and say something about a security deposit. Whatever that meant.

I am living in a shoebox while my mate is gone all day long. The neighbor upstairs stomps around like the carpet is on fire, and someone stinks up the building like human dung every day.

I sank onto Lennox's tiny couch and stared up at the ceiling. I'd built my castle myself, and it was as strong and sturdy as I was. The scents that surrounded me there were wild, free, and natural and did not irritate my nose like those in this place where everyone chose to live in one large house with sections called apartments beside and on top of one another. I couldn't figure out why anyone would choose this given there were so many areas of empty land on which to make a home.

Why is she working so much? Are you running low on treasure, brother? Coming up short?

Dragons amass treasure as a natural instinct. Even when we were exiled and found ourselves in this strange, new world, we continued to collect things that were considered of value in this world—minerals and gems that humans also treasured. Diamonds, gold, platinum, opals, rubies, silver, I had a large cache of stored treasure. I assumed we all had. Although we had difficulties assimilating to certain aspects of the human culture, finance was second nature to us. We found the human financial structure to be primitive and archaic, but we quickly learned to adapt. Each of us carried a healthy investment portfolio as well.

You know I have more treasure than you could even dream of, you old fire-mouth. She wants to work. It is a thing she enjoys. So much that she works all day and works even more when she comes home.

What I wasn't saying was that I seemed to be in the way of her life. She was busy and stumbled over me while trying to get done everything that she needed to get done. While she tried to catch up with Margo and Nance, I was there. When she tried to spread her work out, I was there. Even phone calls were not private. She had spoken on the phone to her parents a few times already, and I had been the subject of the conversation.

Have you talked to her about it?

I growled. *What do you propose I say? I don't like when you leave me all alone? I cannot say that. I am not a youngling. I also refuse to keep her from living her life the way she chooses. She has been bullied by too many as it is.*

Then, I guess you are having difficulties with your mate like Beast, Cezar, and I had. You will figure it out, brother. Would you care to bring her over for dinner tonight?

We must dine at her parents' house tonight. These people... They make our father look like a cuddly youngling's plaything.

His scoff filled my head. *So, they regularly bludgeon and slaughter those who do not do exactly as they command?*

I sighed and cut the connection with him. Squeezing my eyes shut, I was bombarded with the raucous sounds of loud music, a kind called heavy metal, coming from the third floor. It was mixed with an argument from the sixth floor about who ate all the chocolate puffs cereal and put the empty box back on the shelf, an infant's cries on two, a vacuum cleaner on seven, and the idiot upstairs doing a clog dance. I had promised Lennox not to eat any of the tenants in her apartment building. Clearly, I had not thought that through.

Just as I was getting up, I detected Lennox's sweet fragrance approaching. She was home. The tension in my body eased, and a slow smile spread across my face. My mate made everything better. All the irritation, the nasty smells, the jarring, earsplitting cacophony of sounds were manageable with my soft, sweet-smelling Lennox in my arms.

She burst through the front door, carrying her usual two satchels of books and papers with her, and frowned when she saw me. "You're not dressed. Why aren't you dressed?"

Reflexively, I glanced down at myself. Had she gone blind? I was wearing jeans and a T-shirt. I held out my hands and spun. "I am clothed."

She dropped her bags and shook her head, her lips pressed together tightly. "No, dressed for *dinner*." Once again, she was speaking to me as though I was a youngling. "Come on, Remy, you have to dress up a little. And we've gotta hurry. We can't be late or Mom will throw a fit."

"She still frets over whether or not I might eat her. She will be fine."

"That's what you think. Fear won't hold that woman back for long." She rushed past my open arms and disappeared into the bedroom. "I have to change, and I need to do something with my hair. Oh, I have no time!"

I followed, feeling my frustration grow. "You already look beautiful."

"I'm serious, Remy. It was huge that she invited both of us over for dinner. It means she's willing to meet us halfway. And I want her to take us seriously. I want them to like you." She looked up from her vanity for a second and smiled at me. "I missed you."

"Hmph. You do not act as though you missed me." I sat heavily on the bed. "I missed you today, and you are home early."

She rose from her vanity and came to stand in front of me, holding my head against her stomach. "I'm sorry. I'm super stressed. I really want this to go well. I know that my parents are difficult, but they're still my parents, and I guess I'll always feel the need for their approval of us...of *me*. This dinner has a lot riding on it."

Sucking up my frustration, I nodded. "Okay. I do not understand, but I will dress in something else. I will endeavor to be on my best behavior."

She bent over to gently kiss me and groaned when I deepened it. She pulled away quickly. "Later. When we get back."

I removed my nicest pair of jeans out of her closet and a button-up flannel. After putting them on, I sat on the bed and watched as she slipped on a fancy black dress. It clung to her sexy curves. I marveled at her beautiful body. It was perfect, and I was the luckiest dragon that lived to be blessed with such a mate. While I watched, she sat at her vanity and twisted her hair into a fancy, knotted style, which she secured at the nape of her neck. Then, she reapplied her lipstick and met my eyes through the mirror.

She sighed and wrinkled her nose. "I look plain and droll."

"You look stunning. As always."

"I just want them to be proud of me. Someday."

"It's not always best to win the acceptance of certain people." I knew from personal experience. There had been a time when I tried desperately to win the approval of my father—to show him that I was good enough. And for that, my fellow dragons had suffered.

Lennox stood up and turned to face me. "We should get on the road. We have to take my car because we obviously can't fly there."

I bit my tongue. "Fine."

"I'm sorry, Remy. I know you don't understand, but they're my parents. I can't just write them out of my life." She took my hands and stared up at me. "Let's just get through tonight, okay?"

And every dinner like this for the rest of their lives?

Lennox snapped her head away from me and hurried out of the bedroom. "I think they're serving porterhouse. That ought to cheer you up at least."

I followed her out and squeezed into her car, feeling like I was an oversized behemoth stuffing myself into a youngling's toy vehicle. After we were both settled in, she pulled out and headed out of town. I stared out the window and thought vaguely to myself that something needed to change.

Chapter Eighteen

LENNOX

My nerves were frayed. I felt like we were in hostile negotiations with terrorists instead of a family dinner. I'd sat down, and my parents had been fast to claim the seats on either side of me, forcing Remy to circle the table and sit alone. I watched his jaw muscles working, his anger bubbling just under the surface. I wondered how much of it was for me.

Deserved, perhaps. My parents were manipulating and controlling the situation as usual and acting like spoiled children. I never was good at dealing with them, especially when they both worked their machinations on me in unison. They were like gale force winds when they came at me, and I wimped out. I could've gotten up and made a statement by reseating myself next to Remy. As I noticed Remy's expression, I felt even more blameworthy. I'd dragged him into all this. He was only here for me. If I was a better girlfriend to him, maybe I would've told Mom that we weren't ready to come for family dinner. Or maybe I would have laid down the law about how we expected to be treated, or not treated, if we agreed to attend.

The thought of standing up to my mother made my stomach twist in knots. Since the day I was born, I'd viewed her as larger than life, someone not to cross. Frightening.

I regretted not hugging Remy when I first got home. I'd been so stressed about looking acceptable, about pleasing my parents and making them proud, that I'd had difficulty focusing on anything else. I felt ashamed of that. He deserved better.

It was obvious by his expression that he was unhappy. At this point, it was probably just a matter of time before he left me. I had a feeling that things would get complicated out here in the real world and, lord knew, we couldn't live out all our days in paradise. My only solution was to enjoy him while I had him and pray it took a while before he got fed up enough to go. Maybe, if I was a bolder person, I would've told him to go already. I would've put his happiness over mine. But I was selfish, and I wanted him for as long as I could have him.

When Samantha placed the fish course in front of me, she leaned in close and whispered, "A big improvement from the last one." Samantha had worked as the kitchen help for my parents for over two decades. She was a beautiful, round woman with dark hair, now peppered with grey, and skin the color of fresh snow. When I was a small child, I used to think that Snow White probably looked exactly like Samantha. The sweet woman appeared as though she'd never seen the sun a day in her life, but, at sixty, she had no wrinkles to speak of. Her cheeks were smooth as satin, I remembered from all the hugs she'd freely given me as I was growing up. The fact that my parents' still employed staff to care for their home, cook, and serve them dinner in the evenings was ridiculous with just the two of them, but they needed something to make them feel important.

I smiled at Remy across the table and nodded. He was better than David in every way. I wished my parents would see that.

"Remy built his own house, Dad. It's beautiful."

"So, you're a contractor?" My dad cut a piece of fish and cleared his throat. "At least you're employed, I suppose."

"I am not a contractor. I am not employed."

Panic caused my heart rate to increase. Was there no topic that was safe? "He...does other stuff."

"Like threatening innocent people who are just looking out for their daughter's well-being." My mother put her fork down and crossed her knife over it, signaling to Samantha that she was done. "I've lost my appetite."

"Remy has been great around my apartment, too. He even cleans and cooks dinner for me."

Remy took another bite of his fish and stared at me. "I'm also housebroken and do not chew the furniture."

I blushed, embarrassed to have Remy call me out for trying to talk him up like his merits couldn't stand on their own. Trying to explain to Mom and Dad what I saw in Remy, how great he was, was probably futile. He didn't fit into their categories of great. He wasn't a lawyer or an investment banker or from one of the old-money families. He was a freaking dragon. He could fly, and he had a literal stash of gold that could've bought everything my parents owned at least a hundred times over. He was also an amazing guy who fit me so well and made me feel like I was beautiful and vital and sexy and...his *everything*.

"What are you?" Dad pushed his plate away, too. "If you're part... animal...should you really be cohabitating with a human? Why not stick to your own kind?"

Remy took yet another bite of his fish and smiled. "I'm a several-centuries-old dragon. I am not part animal. I am a dragon. Wings, tail, talons, lots of sharp teeth, fire breathing. And my kind is your daughter. She is my mate."

"I think we can all agree that this is ridiculous. You must've performed some kind of New Orleans hocus-pocus trick in the hotel room." Mom slapped Samantha's hands away when she tried to take her wine glass. "Not now, Samantha."

Remy smiled kindly at the woman and handed her his plate. "That was a most deliciously prepared meal. Perhaps you might share the recipe?"

Samantha beamed. "Oh, yes. I'd be delighted. For you, anything." She turned and exited the room with a spring to her step.

When Samantha was gone, Remy put his hands flat on the table and met my mother's stare. In slow motion, his hands grew talons on the table and his eyes burned brighter. The red scales moved across his arms and neck, the veins showed their true golden hue.

Mom and Dad gasped. I put my elbows on the table and held my head in my hands. Remy opened his mouth and revealed a lengthening set of teeth that, according to him, would mark me someday. Not that he'd offered yet.

Casually losing his dragon features just as quickly as they'd appeared, Remy met my eyes and grinned. I watched as he took a deep breath in and flashed those teeth again. I blushed even harder and nearly banged my head on the table when Mom slapped my elbow off it.

"Where are your manners?" Even in the presence of a dragon, Mom couldn't get over herself.

"Lennox, honestly, you're bringing home this...this monster and telling me that he's the man you've chosen? Over a decent, respectable man like David. I think he might take you back, you know." Dad scoffed and threw his napkin down. "Where did we go wrong?"

"This can't be safe. He could eat you, Lenni. There'd be nothing we could do." Mom crossed her arms over her chest. "No one would even believe us."

"There is only one way I plan to ever eat your daughter, and it has nothing to do with hurting her."

"Remy!" I was going to die of embarrassment.

"This is outrageous. Do you hear how he talks to your parents? This cannot work, Lenni. If you need to, you can move back home for a little while. Just until he's gone from the apartment and loses your number."

Remy just stared at me, waiting for me to say something.

"I-I'm happy—"

"He's not human! End of discussion. I'll send Andrew over to get your things tomorrow." Dad pushed away from the table and waved to Samantha on his way out of the room. "Send my dessert to my study."

Mom clapped her hands together once. "It's decided. You'll come back tomorrow. A clean break."

"Mom—"

"Maybe we should send you to therapy, too. Honestly, Lennox, this is a new low, even for you."

"I—"

"And you, *dragon*, or whatever you are, stay away from my daughter or I will involve the authorities. I am determined to see that she has better than you."

Remy stood up and reached into the bag he'd insisted on bringing in with us. He pulled out a stack of gold bars that I hadn't realized he'd been carrying. He tossed them onto the table, making the china rattle, pulled out a couple more and then stepped back. "Lennox, I am returning to the apartment. Are you coming?"

I jumped up. "Are you just going to leave that gold there?"

"Yes. Your parents seem determined to make a profit from their daughter. Maybe that will appease their greed somewhat. I will bring more if that is not satisfactory. I simply hope they will be nicer to you." He took my hand, and still speaking to me, he raised his voice loud enough for it to reverberate around the dining room. "And if anyone shows up to try to remove your belongings tomorrow, or any other time, I will eat them."

Chapter Nineteen

REMY

It was the need to make the claiming special for Lennox that had caused me to wait to mark her. We had talked about what a claiming mark was to a dragon, and how it was done, but the timing had not seemed right. I had been ready the moment I set eyes on her, but mating for a human was different. I'd witnessed enough with my brother and the other mated dragons to know that humans needed time to gradually get used to the idea of mating.

I felt I could wait no longer. There was something happening between us that scared me. As though we were slipping away from each other. I was dismayed by the way she had not confronted her parents, or defended me. That did not feel right. In an attempt to improve our bond, I knew I must officially claim her. No more waiting.

I still needed to make it special in a human way. She'd had a lavish, expensive human mating ceremony set up when she had almost mated the other male—the loser. Dragon claiming marks, on the other hand, were given in private, just between the mated pair, without a huge celebration of friends and family. I planned to create our own celebration and party, just for the two of us, and to make our official claiming special for her in a human way.

Figuring I would keep the claiming a surprise, I discussed with her that I had something special planned for us that evening. I suspected that she guessed my surprise. She wore a look of excitement in her eyes, and the fact that she had put on special, skimpy, lacy undergarments underneath her proper work clothes to tease me and have me drooling all day long told me that she was more than willing to participate.

I thought that she must have felt the oddness between us, too, and was just as desperate as I was for things between us to be okay. She'd agreed to come right home from work.

With the help of many visits back and forth to Cherry, Chyna, and Sky, I spent all morning shopping at the florist, the market, the music store, the confectionery, and a men's clothing store. All afternoon, I was busy preparing things in a way they told me would be romantic and memorable for human females. I purchased filet mignon from the market, a bouquet of roses from the florist, and strawberries dipped in chocolate in a heart-shaped box. I placed candles all around the apartment and fresh sheets on the bed and then covered the sheets in flower petals. As Chyna instructed, I played music from a man named Barry White. I did everything I was told my mate would find romantic. The evening would be special for Lennox, something she would remember forever.

When the meal was cooked and the candles were lit, I dressed in an off-the-rack suit I'd purchased that morning. Lennox would be very surprised and pleased that I "dressed" for dinner. Everything was prepared perfectly.

When Lennox did not come home early as she had promised, I assumed she'd been unable to pull herself away. Perhaps a student needed her help. My Lennox was kind and caring and had a hard time refusing anyone who needed her assistance. When the hour she would normally have been home came and went, I began to worry. I paced the kitchen floor, unsettled and growing increasingly anxious. She came home late frequently, but she would not be late on a special night as this. Would she?

An hour passed.

Our dinner became cold, so I placed it in a warm oven. The candles burned lower.

Another hour passed.

The meal became dry in the oven. The candles became wax stubs. I lost the tie and the jacket.

Another hour.

I put my jeans and T-shirt back on and considered climbing to the roof to transform and scour the city for her. Something might have happened to her. Perhaps she was hurt or injured somewhere.

I warred back and forth between anger and fear. Why had I not gotten one of those cell phones Lennox kept trying to get me to purchase so she could text me when she was going to be late?

Another hour passed.

When the keys finally rattled in the door, I was overcome with extreme relief. I rushed to the door and swung it open before she was able to. I scooped my Lennox into my arms, leaving her keys dangling in the lock. I inspected and sniffed her for injuries as I hugged and squeezed her, reassuring myself that she was alright.

"Wow, oh, okay, hello to you, too." She giggled and hugged me back until she noticed the candle stubs, cold, dry food, and my tie and jacket strewn across the sofa. "Oh, my god. I'm so sorry, Remy! I got stuck at school. Sarah needed help grading papers, and I couldn't say no." She dropped her bags and grimaced apologetically. "I'm so sorry."

A chill swept through me. I released her, stepped away, and leaned against the counter by the fridge. Her words scalded me. Had that truly been what had kept her late and caused me to fret for hours? She looked around the kitchen and living room, taking in the fresh flowers and candles burned down to nothing. "Remy... you did all this?"

I did not answer right away. I needed a moment to calm myself, to discuss things rationally. I had not mentioned to her that I planned to claim her this night, but we had very clearly discussed that I had a special night planned and a surprise for her, and she had promised to arrive home early.

Taking a deep breath, I asked her the question I couldn't understand. The thing I could not wrap my mind around. "Why was tonight different to you?"

Frowning, she tugged her ponytail tighter, a sign that she wanted to change the topic. "What do you mean?"

"When we were invited to dinner at your parents', you could not get home fast enough." I ran my hands through my hair. I was not certain I would like the answer, but I needed one. "What was different? You are telling me that Sarah, or Mandy, or whatever other Susie there is where you work did not ask you for anything that night?"

"I said I'm sorry, Remy. There is no difference. I just...couldn't say no. She really needed help." She came up to me and pressed her palms flat to my chest. "I don't want to fight. Tonight is a special night, right?"

I shook my head again. "No. Tonight is not."

"What?"

"I am not to be used like a piece of furniture. I am angry, Lennox. I have waited and worried for hours that you might be hurt somewhere."

"Ok, that part isn't my fault, Remy! I told you to get a cell phone." Her fingertips pressed into me harder. "I don't want to fight with you. Please, Remy. Let's just go to bed."

"No, Lennox. I want to know why you rush home to go to a dinner that you do not want to go to at your parents' house and you treat tonight like it is not important—not special."

"Tonight is special. I just...I don't know, Remy. Okay? I don't know. I just felt like I couldn't mess up with my parents again. Not after— you know what."

"And it was acceptable with me? Lennox, I have been here every day and every night, waiting for you. You have told me that you want to be here with me, but you never hurry home. I miss you. I miss seeing you and spending time with you."

"Miss me? Remy, I'm here every night!"

"And that is enough for you? The few hours before you fall asleep? Because it is not for me. You wake up and rush around, scurrying out the door, come home tired and hungry, eat, fuck if you are not too tired, sleep, and then wake up and scurry out the door again. You are giving the best Lennox to others, and I have not seen her in a long time."

Her face burned red, and tears filled her eyes. "I can't do this. I can't fight with you."

"What does that mean?"

"I just want to get in bed with you. I want you to hold me and for everything to be okay."

"We cannot just ignore this. We must talk. You have me here sounding like a pathetic loser, begging for you to spend more time with me. I must beg? I simply ask that you value me over the rest of the things in your life. As I value you."

"I can't just quit everything! I have a job and friends, Remy! I have a life! I have responsibilities."

"And they are more important than me, than us?"

"That's not what I said."

"But it is what your actions have implied. You could have told whatever-her-name-is that we had a special night planned. You could have told your mother and father that I was not a monster. You could have been excited to come home and spend time together."

"I can't argue with my mother!" Lennox's eyes narrowed, and she threw up her hands. "Fine. You insist on fighting? Let's fight. I'm fucking exhausted. I'm working sixty hours a week and trying to balance everything, and it is hard on me knowing you're here all day, miserable. Why don't you go out and do something? Maybe you wouldn't miss me so much."

I gritted my teeth. "So, the problem is that I miss you too much?"

"Maybe, it is. Maybe, you're too needy."

Seething, but more hurt than anything, I nodded. "This is how you really feel?"

She looked at her feet and spoke softly. "Maybe, it's better than you haven't marked me yet. I had a feeling this wouldn't work out."

I swallowed a lump of emotion and shook my head at her. "You really feel that way?"

She hesitated and I could see the truth. She was just angry and hurt, too. We both needed space, and I needed to go so I could lick my wounds without becoming any more pathetic.

"I will leave."

Chapter Twenty

LENNOX

"Wait, Remy..."

He only hesitated once, momentarily, when he got to the door and pulled it open. "We have said enough angry things for this night."

I stood frozen, shell shocked, until I felt the first tear roll down my cheek. What had I done? I told my feet to run after him, but I was scared. I'd snapped at him, and I was wrong. I wanted to talk to him, but I would have to face how mean I'd been to him, and how unfair.

I sat down heavily at the kitchen table and looked around. Candle stubs were everywhere. Flowers, food. Soft music played in the background. Barry White, if I wasn't mistaken. That was impressive in itself. Remy hadn't even been able to get music to play before. He had a little difficulty with the smart home system. There was a box of chocolate-covered strawberries. Melting. He'd done so much to make the night special.

I rested my forehead on the table and groaned. I'd really messed up. No wonder he was angry. Hurt. He was more hurt than angry. And with good reason. I'd ruined the evening he'd worked so hard on.

Maybe there was still time to get him back inside and do something to make it up to him. I would figure out the right words to say to make it better and it would all be okay. I raced to the door and ran down the stairway that led to the parking lot, looking frantically in every direction.

"Remy!"

Jerry, my downstairs neighbor, sat up from his patio chair. "You looking for the big guy?"

"Yeah. Where'd he go?"

He took a long pull from a joint and whistled. "I think this shit is laced. I swear I saw him turn into a red pterodactyl and fly away. This is some good shit right here."

Deflating, I felt my entire body slump. "Thanks, Jerry."

Upstairs, I closed myself in. I passed through to the bedroom to change out of my work clothes and stopped. More candles. Rose petals sprinkled over the sheets. Ugh, I sank into the pillows and groaned.

Maybe he'd be back in the morning and we'd laugh about our first big fight. I would explain to him that often it was impossible to say no to people at work. He was my first priority, but my reputation as an educator was at stake. He had to understand that. He'd see.

Only, he didn't come back in the morning. When I left for work, he still wasn't back. I left the door unlocked, afraid to lock him out if he came back while I was gone. While I was at work, I called Jerry twice to ask if he'd seen Remy. Nothing. I stayed after work to help Monica with a banner she was making for the upcoming pep rally, even though all I wanted to do was run home and see if Remy had returned. Inside, I already knew...

He hadn't.

I went to bed that night holding his pillow and shedding tears all over it. He wasn't back the next morning, either. Still, I left the door unlocked and hoped I'd find him there when I got home. It was my day to stay late to help with dismissal and then the science club, but I knew he still wouldn't be there when I got home.

Another night spent alone.

Another morning waking up alone. And I felt even worse. Every day the loneliness, the feeling of isolation and abandonment, grew worse.

Why was I suddenly so lonely? Before I'd met Remy, when I was engaged to David, I always slept alone and never felt lonely. Now, I was not only lonely, but it was also as though a piece of me was missing.

At first, I had so much hope that he was coming back once he cooled off that my fear didn't have room to grow. By the third morning of waking up alone, my fear had grown into a creature with its own heartbeat that took up space in my apartment. In response, I stayed even later at work, because at least there I could somewhat distract myself. Of course, Remy was coming back. We were mates.

After spending the week alone, the fear crowded me and was beginning to bully me and shove me around. I had no way of getting in contact with Remy. Well, except going to his place.

Maybe he was just taking some time to cool off. Maybe he was just hanging out with his twin and his other dragon guy friends. Or maybe...maybe he wasn't coming back. Ever.

I supposed I could go to his castle. I wasn't exactly sure I could find it. I'd stayed with him at his place for two weeks, but we'd flown in and flown out. I wasn't horrible with directions, and if I was hard pressed, I thought maybe I could find it...somewhere...in the middle of a swamp. But what if I went there and he was still mad? What if he yelled or screamed or ignored me or worse... What if he told me that he no longer had feelings for me and asked me kindly to leave? Ugh, I couldn't face the possibility.

It was around this time that I slipped into a mourning phase.

When Margo texted me at work and insisted that she and Nance were stopping over that evening, I was too depressed to argue. Besides, it was a way to fill the empty space. I got home from another long day and shoved a frozen lasagna in the oven. I had time to clear away the melted candle stubs and dying flowers that were still out before they got there.

Margo burst in with the usual subtly of a bull in a china shop. "Where's Remy? We wanted to discuss his dragon friends with him. It's not fair that you get all the red-hot dragon loving to yourself...see what I did there? Red-hot!"

Nance looked around. "Hold up. No, really. Where is Remy? He's always here."

I meant to answer, but when I opened my mouth, I just started sobbing.

"Oh, honey!" Margo hurried over and pulled me into her arms. "What happened?"

Nance was like a hound dog. She immediately searched the bedroom, fridge, and lastly, the trash can where she found the wilted flowers and candle stubs. "Uh-oh."

Margo frowned. "What are you doing, weirdo? Get out of the trash can."

"I'm investigating. Look what I found in here. The remnants of candles and dead, dried-up flowers."

"Why are you investigating the trash can?"

"It's effective, isn't it?"

Margo rolled her eyes and ushered me into a chair. "Talk."

"Remy left. I don't think he's coming back." I folded my arms on the table and let my forehead sag down onto them. "It's all my fault."

"I don't believe that for a second. You're an angel. Tell us everything." She sat down beside me and rested her chin on her fist. "*Everything.*"

Chapter Twenty-One
REMY

Blaise flew in and sat next to me on the patio, his naked ass the last thing I wanted to see. "You have been ignoring me."

"And yet, here you are. You did not take the hint?"

"What is wrong with you, and where is your mate?"

"Home."

"Why?"

I groaned and sank down farther in my chair. "Because we...we are..."

He made a face. "What?"

"Come on, brother. I do not want to get into this." And I really didn't. I had been doing my best to just make it through the past few days. It was everything I could do not to fly back to Lennox.

"Not an option. You came to my castle and forced me to talk all the time when I was trying to win Chyna."

"You called me over, ashhead."

"Same difference. I can feel you going through sorrow. Talking feels better." He groaned at his own words. "Father would be ashamed of us."

I snorted and dipped into my sarcasm. "Yes, look at us not beating our mates to keep them in line. Such shameful sons."

"So, why is she there and you are here?"

I blew out a rough breath and shrugged. "I do not know."

"Bullshit."

"We had an argument. I am doing as Cezar suggested and giving her a human thing called *space*."

He rolled his eyes. "Stupid. Go get her."

I looked out across the water. "It is not that easy, brother. She is not ready, I think. She is afraid of confronting things and just keeps quiet. She allows people to treat her poorly—and then she blows up at me! *Me*."

"I am still not following why you left her there."

"You would not understand."

"Try me."

I growled. "Chyna desires you all the time. I have seen her, even when she is enjoying herself with other people. She looks for you in the room and always circles back to you as soon as she can. She *wants* to be with you. Lennox... She does not seem to want that. She stays away from me, and she does everything she can to remain at work instead of coming home to be with me. I am unwanted."

"You sound like the females in all those stupid romance movies Chyna makes me watch."

"You sound like an ashhead." I stood up and walked out on the dock over to the water. I thought a swim might help, but I did not feel like jumping in. I just sat on the edge and dipped my feet in the water.

"Sorry. You do not sound like a female—that much."

I made a face. "You still sound like an ashhead."

"Remy, go to her. Talk to her."

"I tried. Now, I am doing *space*. Perhaps she will realize she misses me...like I miss her." I frowned. "I confess, it is much harder than it sounded. I had hoped she would have come here by now. I had hoped she would have stopped me from leaving in the first place. But she did not. Maybe she does not feel the same bond with me as I feel with her."

"Are we really going to do this? Seriously? Of course, she does. You are mates. Like the rest of us, bound together, perfect for each other, blah, blah, blah. All the same stuff you said to me about Chyna. And you were right."

I had said all those things, but somehow it seemed different now that I was going through it and feeling like my chest was being crushed under a boulder.

But Blaise did have a point. I would not be able to stay away much longer. Fuck space. Part of me wished she would come to me and show me that I was important to her.

"Don't be stubborn for too long, brother. I regret every minute I gave up with Chyna."

"Do you want a beverage?"

He laughed. "Not at all. I want to go home to my mate and make love to her before she falls asleep watching some boring plant show on television. But you are my kin, and I am here for you. That is why I had Armand stop by his castle to pick up some of his special brew. He will be here soon."

I nodded and lay back on the dock. "Just pour it into my mouth until I pass out."

"What if Lennox never arrives? What if she is home waiting for you to come to her and wondering why you do not love her the way she loves you?"

"She never said she loves me."

"Did you tell her?"

"Well, no. I told her she is my mate. That is the same."

Blaise laughed. "You have much to learn. Start with watching movies called rom-coms."

"You think she does not know that I love her?"

Blaise looked up and nodded in greeting to Armand as he flew in. "I think we assume a lot as dragons."

I took the flask Armand handed to me and swore. "Why is this so difficult?"

Armand shrugged. "I would not know. I have been to every bar in the area no less than four times. I've been to church. I've been to the library. I've been to crocheting classes, and I have even done something called wedding crash—attending the mating ceremony of humans that I don't know. Nothing. I do have a very nice scarf, and I am working on an afghan, though. And I learned a dance called the Macarena."

I took a long pull from the flask and shrugged back at him. "I hate to break it to you, but it would seem that finding a mate is the easy part. It is afterward that you will want to ram your skull into the side of a mountain. Repeatedly."

Blaise laughed. "Ignore him. He is boohooing like a youngling thinking his mate does not love him and does not spend enough time with him."

Armand scowled. "You are supposed to be the twins of the bloodiest kingdom on record, sired by the most brutal ruler in the old world. By fire, the two of you are pathetic."

Blaise and I gave each other a look. "He will understand when he meets his mate."

"I would be grateful to simply find a mate to stop this ticking time bomb over my head. The eclipse is not far off. Less than a year and you will be pushing me into the lake with cinder blocks tied to my ankles. I saw that in a movie about a group of humans called the mafia."

I grimaced. "I am not pushing you into *my* lake. You would come back and haunt me."

Blaise sat down next to me, and I handed him the flask. "You have both been watching too much television."

"Yes, well. That's another thing that's different in this world. That box called television is always present, and there is always something to watch. I learn much from it." Armand held up his brew. "The idea for this batch was from the television. Kind of."

"This batch is from hell. Do not lie, brother. Is this the same batch that made me fly into the side of a building?"

He nodded. "It is a good recipe. We must finish it before Ovide asks for more, though. It puts him in a sour mood."

"What else is new?"

Chapter Twenty-Two

LENNOX

"This is the last place I want to be, Margo." It was a Saturday night, and her bar was busy. I was happy for her that her business had such a great volume of traffic, but why she had to drag me to it, I didn't understand. People kept getting too close to me, and for the first time in my life, I found myself wanting to elbow and pick fights with people. I was considering actually doing it, too.

"Yet, here you are." She all but shouted at me as she rushed around, slinging beers to people.

I frowned. "Should I have stayed home?"

She stopped, put her hands on her hips, and looked me in the eye. "You should have done what you wanted to do."

I opened my mouth to say something back and then snapped it shut. Why hadn't I? "You made me come," I offered feebly.

Margo stared at me for a second longer, with raised brows, then went back to wiping the bar down with a rag. "You're a big girl, Len. All you had to do was voice your own opinion."

She had a point. I had a habit of going along with what everyone else wanted, even at the cost of my own comfort. I *had* wanted to stay home. Sure, I would have spent the evening crying into Remy's pillow, but even that was preferable to sitting in a bar surrounded by drunken assholes.

"I should probably go home."

"If that's what you want." She snagged someone's debit card and waved it at me. "It's about time you do what you want, Lenni. In everything. If you want Remy, go get him. If you don't, keep hiding from him. Your choice."

I frowned. "It's not that easy."

"Yes, it is. What do you want?"

A guy with a bald head and a neck tattoo leaned over the bar. "I want a damn beer!"

Margo glared and shook her finger at him. "You yell at me again mister and you'll be picking your teeth up off the floor."

I stifled a laugh and stood up. "I want to go home."

"Then go. I'll call you and check on you tomorrow."

I left her to her bartending and drove home lost in thought. As I drove, it became apparent why Margo had dragged me there in the first place. It had been a ploy to show me that I needed to be more vocal and assert myself. She was clever-sneaky that way, and as much as it could annoy me, I loved her for caring. I thought again about her words. *It's about time you do what you want, Lenni.* What did I want?

Besides Remy. I didn't need to think hard to figure out that I wanted Remy. But what else? I wanted a happy life. I wanted to be married to him with kids. A lot of kids. I wanted to watch our kids grow up together and enjoy all of the phases they went through while Remy and I grew older together. Not exactly old, with the antiaging thing that Remy told me dragons had going on. I wanted to be able to see my parents without feeling so much pressure. I wanted to be able to stand up for myself and say what I felt. I wanted to be able to say no when I felt like saying no.

But where to start? How would I find the strength to speak my mind and stop allowing people to push me around? Because I needed to at least take some progressive steps in that direction if I wanted things with Remy to work. I could go to him and tell him how I was feeling, but he deserved more. He deserved for me to show him he was important to me—through my actions. First, I needed to be able to show myself, through my actions, that I valued *me*. I couldn't convince him that he was valued without first learning to value and defend myself.

I got home and settled onto my couch with my kindle, searching through the most current and highly rated self-help books. I ended up downloading a guide to assertiveness for women entitled *A Bitch with Boundaries*. I spent an embarrassingly long time pouring over it and making notes.

I was excited to be taking a proactive approach to my life and relationship...if I still had one...if there was any chance of getting Remy back...if Remy hadn't walked away for good.

I fell asleep on the couch and then spent all of Sunday studying and practicing what I'd learned through visualization. I tried not to feel too pathetic that I needed to read a book and study it to be able to stand up to people, or express my own wants and needs, but I'd never learned how to do it. According to the book, it was normal for someone who had been raised with pushy, domineering parents like mine.

Come Monday morning, I had to skip breakfast due to the nausea that had a vice grip on my stomach. It was embarrassing that I was close to throwing up simply because of anxiety over having to put into practice what I'd learned about setting boundaries and being more assertive.

It would start with Sarah. She was nice enough, but she always asked me to do extra stuff for her. She never went to anyone else. I knew she wasn't choosing me because we were such great friends. We weren't. I knew she wasn't choosing me because the "helping out" was reciprocal. It wasn't. Some of the times I "helped" her, she didn't even hang around. She just dumped her work on me and left.

According to the gossip grapevine, she was hooking up with Mike Jenkins, the gym coach, and I suspected they were sneaking away during school hours. While I did her work. Hey, I didn't judge her for wanting to be with her man, if that was the case, but I'd been giving up time with my mate to help her out. Because I was too much of a pushover to say no.

That had to end. There was a list of names in my purse. Number one on it was Sarah. *Dealing with her was step one to becoming the woman Remy deserved*, I reminded myself.

My stomach knotted more the longer the day went on. I knew exactly what was coming. I'd seen Sarah glance my way multiple times in the teacher's lounge, but she never approached me when other educators could overhear her. According to the book, I was a people pleaser, programmed by my parents to please. I was determined to become a bitch with boundaries, though, no matter how much my stomach hurt.

When Sarah finally approached me, I panicked. She opened her mouth to speak, and I cut her off like a mad person. "No!"

She stepped back, her eyes wide. "Sorry?"

I cleared my throat and forced a smile. "I can't stay late or do anything for you, Sarah."

Her returned smile was as brittle as mine. "That's okay. I was going to ask about tomorrow. If that's a problem..."

That hanging sentence would've normally cracked me. I hated the negative space of conversations, especially when people looked at me with so much expectation. I forced my head to shake back and forth. "Not tomorrow, either."

"Oh, do you have something else going on?"

I twisted my fingers together behind me and squeezed. "I just don't want to."

"O-kay." Her lips pressed together tightly and she nodded. "That's fine. You can still help me with grading my papers, right? I'm swamped. I wish I had a free period every day like you. It must be easy to keep up with your work with a free period every day, right?"

My smile slipped, and those knots in my stomach rose up as a sourness in my throat. I was getting angry, though. I'd been blowing off Remy to help the woman in front of me, who was so quick to insult me and become nasty when I refused to bend over backward for her. "I can't grade your papers, actually, Sarah. Maybe you can ask someone else."

"I can't ask anyone else. They're all busy, too."

I forced myself to walk to my desk and grab my purse. "I should get going. I have dinner with my parents."

"Ugh... Are you really not going to help me anymore, Lennox? Seri-ously? That's kind of selfish."

Pausing in the doorway, I forced myself to fight back tears. I was so angry that I wanted to scream at her, but I just had to stand my ground, and I'd be free of her. *Bitch with boundaries, bitch with bound-aries, bitch with boundaries,* I mentally chanted. "If by selfish you mean standing up for myself and setting boundaries, then yes, I am being selfish. Super-duper, stinkin' selfish. That's me. Deal with it."

In the parking lot, I called my mom right away and continued the momentum. As soon as she answered, I jumped in, "I'm not coming to dinner tonight. You were so rude to Remy the last time, and I love him. If you and Dad insist on treating him that way, we won't be back. Ever."

Breathing heavily, my heart pounding, I waited for her response. I was trembling. Terrified. I was always terrified of messing up with them. Their love always felt so conditional.

"Fine, Lennox. You're coming next week. Bring the monst—*Remy.*"

Great. I got her to accept my conditions, and I wasn't even sure I could get Remy back or, if I did, he'd agree to going to dinner at my parents' again. But my assertiveness worked, and I wasn't about to stop there. "One word, one negative word to him and we're out of there."

She hesitated. There was an awkward silence. "We'll see you next week."

"Talk to you next week." I was starting to cry. I had to hang up despite the fact that she continued.

"Where did he get all that gold, Lennox? Is his family well off?"

"See you then,'" I sing-songed.

I heard her quick reply before I disconnected, "Don't forget to bring him."

Chapter Twenty-Three

REMY

"This is the spot?" Blaise looked around at the plot of land we stood on and nodded. "It is a good location and has plenty of water."

Beast, Cezar, and Ovide stood next to him, taking everything in. We were all looking out over the plot of land I'd purchased. A hundred acres, close to Lennox's school, with a lake and enough trees to be cleared that I could build a nice dwelling with the lumber without having to cart in too many new materials and supplies.

"I'm going to build the castle on that hill, so it will overlook our territory." I tugged the drawing I'd made out of my pocket and held it up. "I wish I had settled here when we first arrived in this world. I would have been closer to her all along."

"Well, she's only been alive for twenty-nine years, so it has probably all worked out for the best." Blaise elbowed me. "I get what you mean, though. I felt the same when I found how close Chyna had been to me all along."

Ovide cleared his throat and looked at my drawing. "Really? You are building your castle based on a crayon drawing?"

I pulled it away from him. "Ashbreath. I'm going to draw up professional plans once I go over everything with Lennox to be sure what she wants. She will probably want a large walk-in closet like the females on those house-hunting shows."

"Or, maybe, you will want a large closet to store all your emotions." Blaise laughed when I punched him and then punched me back.

I grabbed him around his neck and held him bent over at my side while he fought himself free. "I can kick your tail. Don't forget that."

He swung his leg, taking me down, and we wrestled for a while, then we all took a long swim in the lake before flying back home.

In the evening, there would be another of their get-togethers. When I declined the invitation, I was informed by the females that my refusal to attend was not accepted as the gathering would be held at my castle. Great.

Ovide and Armand were exempt from having to attend, but apparently, I was the target of their well-meaning torture.

My dragon still raged. He was furious that we were doing this thing called *space*. Frankly, I hated it as well. I had hoped Lennox would show up for me, but it had not happened, and I was not going to stay away much longer. I missed her too much.

Purchasing the land closer to her work was a solution to the problems we were having. I would be working on constructing the new castle during the days. This would keep me from sitting around the small cagelike apartment, missing her day long, in the midst of the cacophony of human smells and sounds that wreaked havoc with my senses. I would still not like being away from her all day, but it would be tolerable. If I could not spend more time with her, I would accept what she could offer me.

———

Cezar flew in with Cherry sitting in a harness atop him. The other dragons always gave him grief about the harness, but he would not back down. She was huge, due at any time, and her large belly made her awkward. He insisted she be strapped in for safety. I couldn't blame the dragon. I would be as protective with my mate. And, although they teased, I suspected the others would, too. Mentally, I formulated a picture of how Lennox might look if she was pregnant. Incredibly sexy, I decided.

Blaise and Cherry arrived, carrying cupcakes, steaks, and baked potatoes for the grill, seconds before Beast showed up with his family.

Sky, Nick, and Casey all rode on Beast's back as though he was a large, black dragon bus. Their arms were loaded with salad, chips, hamburgers, hotdogs, and soda. Great. I would never get rid of them.

Beast blew flames to set the grill alight, and they all scurried around preparing a feast while I moped that my mate was not with me. I was regretting choosing to go along with this giving of *space*.

Throughout the evening, as everyone stuffed their faces, the focus was on Cherry's belly. Turns were taken to rub it and to feel the youngling from inside her kick at hands placed on her stomach. No one was certain how long her gestation would be since no human, that we knew of, had ever conceived a dragon youngling, but it seemed clear that her time was nearing an end.

After everyone ate, Blaise uncovered sweets.

"Blaise made his special cupcakes. He's so good in the kitchen," Chyna grinned. "I think I've gained five pounds from his baked goods alone."

I tried to imagine my father seeing Blaise baking and cooking, for a female no less, and laughed to myself at how red faced and frothing at the mouth in anger he would have been. Our sire had tried his hardest to make a ruthless, bloodthirsty ruler out of us both. It served him right to spend whatever afterlife he was in watching Blaise bake for his mate and me become emotional over mine.

Cherry moaned as she shoved half a cupcake into her mouth. Cezar shifted in his seat in response to her groan of pleasure, clearly enjoying his mate's reaction. "So delicious. I love cupcakes. Can we take home the extras?"

"They are for you, anyway," Blaise grinned. "Take them."

She pouted. "That's so sweet. I'd hug you, but the baby has made Cezar extra possessive. He's likely to char you."

"I will do more than char any male who puts his hands on my Cherry."

Sky moved onto Beast's lap and smiled. "This was a great barbecue. Whose turn is it to host next week? Everyone at our place?"

Casey piped up, "Yeah, and Cezar, we can have a gaming marathon. Bring your controller."

Nick nodded. "That sounds awesome."

Cezar grinned and pulled Cherry closer. When her oversized belly blocked him from holding her as close as he wanted to, he just lifted her and plopped her on his lap, hugging her to his chest.

Blaise met my eyes over Chyna's head and smiled before communicating telepathically. *My mate is with child.*

My heart expanded, pure happiness flooding me. I was going to be an uncle. I reached over and punched his arm in congratulations before giving Chyna a side hug. She was a good new sister. "You are going to have your hands full keeping this one in line."

She blushed and turned to punch Blaise in the thigh. "You said I could be the one to announce it."

"Announce what?" Cherry's ears perked up.

Chyna shook her head. "Nothing."

I laughed and stood up. "I'm getting more brew. Anyone need anything?"

The low *hum* of a motor coming closer drowned out what Blaise was saying to me. The hair on the back of my neck prickled. I scanned the horizon and watched as a boat came into view. I knew instantly it was Lennox, even before I caught her scent on the wind, and dropped the flask I'd been holding.

Chyna squinted. "Who's that?"

I stood and jogged down the dock where I watched, waiting for her boat to pull up. I'd felt every second of every minute away from her like a dagger to my chest, but seeing her boat racing full speed toward me sent the fire in my veins pulsing through me.

Instead of slowing down and pulling up to the dock, though, she swung the boat wildly, heading for land full speed ahead, gesturing wildly to me with a frantic expression. Instinct took over in a beat. I shifted and launched myself toward her using my long talons to pluck her from the boat seconds before it crashed into a cypress grove bordering the bank of the lake.

Terrified that she was hurt, I landed us both on sturdy ground and shifted, grabbing her arms, and looked her over in a mad panic. "Are you alright? What happened?"

She was trembling, and it took me a couple of nervous seconds to realize she had collapsed into a fit of giggles. "I'm so sorry. I don't really know how to drive these things. It was my first time. I..."

I stopped and stared at her while her giggling fit continued.

"This boat rental guy refused to give me a ride from the marina near my apartment. He was a jerk about it, so I took his boat. He's probably behind me. I'm sorry! I just wanted to get here, and I wouldn't take no for an answer."

"You stole a boat?"

"And, whew, that was a close call! I thought I was going to have to bail by jumping into the water, but I wasn't sure I'd be able to jump far enough from the boat, and I was thinking about my hair getting caught in those blade thingies. I don't look good with short hair. I might be freaking out a little." She giggled some seconds more before she suddenly stopped and sucked in a big breath. "Yes. I stole a boat!"

Chapter Twenty-Four

LENNOX

I'd lost my mind.

I realized that then, especially since Remy was staring at me like I'd grown a second set of limbs. But that didn't matter to me as much as getting Remy back mattered.

"I needed to get here, and I'm trying this thing where I'm being what's called a *boundaried bitch* and asserting myself by telling people what I want, or by saying no. No is a big one. I have a list of names in my purse for people who are getting an automatic NO. Anyway, the boat rental guy wouldn't listen to me. And he was rude. So, when his back was turned, I hopped in and took off. I'll pay him later.

I suppose, looking back, that might not have been the best way to handle the situation, but I was dying to see you. I couldn't wait a second longer." I heaved another huge breath and hurried on with my nervous rambling before I was interrupted. "I'm so sorry, Remy. I was wrong. You've always supported me and stood up for me, and I should have done the same for you. By being a wimp and not forcing myself to confront people who were taking advantage of me, I was inadvertently putting them first. I swear that you're so much more important to me than them—than anyone. I'm still working on my self-improvement, but I promise I'm getting better and I'm going to keep trying hard. I mean, there I was doing favors for a coworker who doesn't even like me and trying to please parents who are miserable and will never be satisfied. Stupid."

A man who looked almost identical to Remy, minus the beard, walked over, a huge grin spread across his face. "We are all leaving so that the two of you may be alone."

Remy nodded emphatically without taking his eyes off me. "Yes. Great. Get out of here."

I held my hand out to the guy, who was obviously Remy's twin, and tried to look sane. "Hi. I'm Lennox. Nice to meet you."

Remy growled and pulled me into his chest. "Not right now."

The guy laughed. "He will not allow another male close to you for a while. He has been missing you. A lot." The guy patted Remy on the shoulder. "Chyna and I will take care of the male at the boat rental. Ugh...the male who *used* to have a boat to rent, that is. I am Blaise, by the way."

"You're the twin." I twisted my head around to look at the boat that was no longer in the water and was now up against a tree. "If you're returning the boat, will you just toss my purse out on the dock first?"

He laughed. "That boat is not going anywhere. It is, as you humans say, *totaled*."

Remy squeezed me tighter and growled at his twin again, which I assumed was a warning to stop talking to me and go away. At any rate, it made me giggle. He turned my face to his and kissed me softly. I was so relieved that he wasn't pushing me away. I wound my arms around his neck and held on to him, kissing him back the way I'd been wanting to since he walked out.

I pulled back and looked around. When I was nearing his place, I'd noticed a group of people, but everyone was gone. The remnants of a barbecue were left behind. "I'm sorry I interrupted your party. They—"

Remy kissed down my neck and nibbled my tender skin. "They are not important. You are."

I moaned and stroked his hair. He was so quick to put me before anyone or anything. I was incredibly lucky and still felt guilty for allowing him to think he wasn't equally as important to me. "Remy, I need to apologize more."

He pulled away enough to yank my shirt over my head. My bra came off just as fast. With his hands cupping my breasts, he leaned down and sucked one nipple into his mouth before moving to the next one. "I do not need more apology. I need more of you. I have waited long enough."

Shivering against him, I moaned as his teeth nipped and nibbled and his tongue laved.

Suddenly, remembering where I was, I stood on my toes to try to glimpse over his shoulder and make sure no partygoers were lingering and getting a peepshow.

"Gone. They are gone." He lifted me by my ass and walked us toward the table that his friends had just been seated around. "Missed you so much."

Even though they cleared out mighty fast, I trusted him when he said they were all gone and let him lay me back on the table. I knocked over a salad bowl, landed on a pack of hot dog buns, and was pretty sure some lettuce leaves were sticking to my back, but it didn't matter. I needed him. I wanted him. My body was demanding its connection with him just as much as his seemed to be. "I shouldn't have let you go. I should have tried harder to stop you..."

He slid my jeans and underwear off in one go and knelt in front of me. Burying his face between my thighs, he devoured me, running his tongue over my wet folds, sucking my clit into his mouth, feasting on me as though he was starving for me.

In minutes, he had me screaming as an orgasm slammed into me, fast and furious. I gripped the sides of the tables and held on, tossing my head from side to side, as waves of pleasure curled my toes and had my eyes rolling. Remy continued to plunge it into me and lap up all my juices.

When he raised his head, I tried to get control of myself, but I didn't have a chance. His thick shaft entered me, sliding deeper and deeper. My back arched and he slipped his arm under me, pulling me up so he could hold on to me tightly while he thrust. Hard and fast, he pumped.

I held onto his neck with one arm and used the other to reach behind me to get leverage so I could rock my hips back into him. With every thrust, his cock hit all my sensitive nerve endings, filling me deeper than I would have thought possible. My head fell back on my neck like it was rubber. Remy's mouth was on my nipples, every nibble, suck, and bite firing off tingles of white-hot pleasure.

He looked into my eyes and cradled the back of my head so I would be forced to look at him. "I love you, and I am going to claim you and mark you as mine forever."

Maybe it was the intensity of his words that triggered my biggest orgasm yet, or maybe not, but I screamed as my walls tried to close around him. I felt him swell and harden even more, somehow, and he was saying something, but I couldn't focus on what it was, not as my blood rushed through me and sounded like a drumbeat in my ears. Then, he tilted my head to the side. I watched as his teeth lengthened and sharpened. As our mutual orgasms continued to pulse, he sank his teeth into the sensitive flesh of my neck. It felt as though a circle was completing.

Everything went out of focus as the feeling of soaring through space at a hundred miles an hour hit me. Pleasure tickled me at that moment, feeling like a hundred little hands, tongues, and fingers stroking, licking, and pleasing. My orgasm strengthened and rolled into something I'd never felt. Never ending. A whole-body orgasm.

Remy's seed filled me, hotter and fuller than ever. His tongue lapped at the bite on my neck, his low growl filling my ears. His hands were everywhere. I didn't know what was holding us down from just floating up into the sky.

I was claimed.

I didn't know how much time had passed, but the sun had set, the mosquitoes were out, and it was getting chillier. Remy scooped me up and carried me inside to his bathroom where he put us both in a hot shower. Somehow, he found the energy to make love to me again. Slowly, lazily. Another few orgasms later, I lost count, we ended up in his bed, wrapped up in each other, under his blankets.

I might've napped. I felt like I was still floating somewhere with him, lost in our own world. "Are we on a cloud?"

"If you would like to rest on a cloud, I will fly you up to rest on a cloud. Anything you wish."

I kissed his chest and sighed. "That...is...everything."

His deep chuckle vibrated my chest. "You wanted to talk when you arrived and I did not let you talk."

"No worries. That was so much better than talking."

"It was pretty fucking amazing." He kissed the mark that was still raw and torn and growled. "You are mine, mate."

Smiling, I nodded. "You love me."

"I love you so much. And I should have said those words before." He took my hand in his and kissed my ring finger. "I wish to marry you. It is not a dragon thing, but I want to do this human thing and be your husband. Please."

Tears filled my eyes, and I sat up. "You want to marry me?"

He grinned. "Yes. A lot. I bought a ring."

"Ahhhh! Show me!" Clearing my throat and trying again, I spoke calmly. "I mean, can I see it?"

He reached into the nightstand beside the bed and pulled out a ring box. "It is not the only thing I bought."

"Wait. Before you give me that or tell me anything else, I have to tell you something." When he paused, I pushed my shoulders back and reached up to brush my hair out of my face. "I'm serious about showing you that you're my priority. I don't want us to live in that apartment anymore. I know you hate it. From now on, we'll live here, and I'll commute from here in the mornings. I am not going to work late anymore, either. And...I love you, too."

Grinning from ear to ear, he pulled me against him and captured my mouth with his in a deep kiss. When he pulled back, his huge grin returned. "I purchased land. Closer to your school. I am going to build us a new castle—with whatever design specifications that you want— and it will be our home. We can have younglings, pets, whatever you desire."

"You're building us a house?!"

"A *big* house. On a large piece of land, so no more shoebox living. We can walk around naked and make love anywhere, and you can scream as loud as you want without fearing that the neighbors will hear you. It also has a big lake that we can swim in." He nipped my chin. "And fuck in."

"You want children?" I was mush, I was pretty sure.

"Yes. I would love to have many younglings. Many little females who look like you and many little males who hopefully don't act like Blaise and me." He pushed my hair out of my face and smiled sweetly, showing the cute dimple in his left cheek just above his beard line. "I want everything with you from now on. You are my mate."

"I'm sorry for everything before. I was just—"

"It does not matter. I will never give you space again. I should not have done so the first time."

"It's a nonissue because I'm never letting you walk out again. You're *mine*, mate."

He pulled us both up and held the ring box out to me. "Will you be my wife, too?"

I opened it and felt my eyes go wide. "Holy fuck." The thing had to be about eight karats.

Laughing, he pulled it out and slipped it onto my finger. "Hmmm, perhaps it is not our offspring behaving like *me* that will be a problem. You are stealing boats and, how is that saying? Cursing like a sailor?"

I gaped at the rock on my finger. "Remy, this is... like, ginormous!"

"Well?"

I clasped the rock to my chest. "What do you mean, well?"

"Does this mean we will have our human mating ceremony?"

"Of course! With or without the ring, that's a given."

He pulled me into his lap and offered his fist, his little finger extended. I stared at it for a second before it dawned on me. I wrapped my own finger around his. And, just like that, I had it all—the dragon, the castle, the sparkling diamond, and a pinky promise that guaranteed me my fairytale happily ever after.

THE END

NEXT BOOK IN THIS SERIES...

When Armand meets Angel, he knows she's not his mate.
She can't be—she's pregnant with another male's child.
Yet, no female has ever claimed his heart as she has.

Angel of Death is cursed.
Everyone around her dies.
The trick, she's learned, is to never get close to anyone.
Damned if she hasn't screwed that up, and her screwup may endanger the lives
of the two people she cares for the most—the man she's trying desperately not to
fall in love with, and her own newborn daughter.

Armand is willing to give up eternal life to spend what little time he has left
with Angel.
The only problem is, if he dies, Angel will take the blame.

P.O.L.A.R.

(**P**rivate **O**ps: **L**eague **A**rctic **R**escue) is a specialized, private operations task force—a maritime unit of polar bear shifters. Part of a world-wide, clandestine army comprised of the best of the best shifters, P.O.L.A.R.'s home base is Siberia...until the team pisses somebody off and gets re-assigned to Sunkissed Key, Florida and these arctic shifters suddenly find themselves surrounded by sun, sand, flip-flops and palm trees.

1. Rescue Bear
2. Hero Bear
3. Covert Bear
4. Tactical Bear
5. Royal Bear

———

BEARS OF BURDEN

In the southwestern town of Burden, Texas, good ol' bears Hawthorne, Wyatt, Hutch, Sterling, and Sam, and Matt are livin' easy. Beer flows freely, and pretty women are abundant. The last thing the shifters of Burden are thinking about is finding a mate or settling down. But, fate has its own plan...

1. Thorn
2. Wyatt
3. Hutch
4. Sterling
5. Sam
6. Matt

———

SHIFTERS OF HELL'S CORNER

In the late 1800's, on a homestead in New Mexico, a female shifter named Helen Cartwright, widowed under mysterious circumstances, knew there was power in the feminine bonds of sisterhood. She provided an oasis for those like herself, women who had been dealt the short end of the stick. Like magic, women have flocked to the tiny town of Helen's Corner ever since. Although, nowadays, some call the town by another name, **Hell's Crazy Corner.**

1. Wolf Boss
2. Wolf Detective
3. Wolf Soldier
4. Bear Outlaw
5. Wolf Purebred

———

DRAGONS OF THE BAYOU

Something's lurking in the swamplands of the Deep South. Massive creatures exiled from their home. For each, his only salvation is to find his one true mate.

1. Fire Breathing Beast
2. Fire Breathing Cezar
3. Fire Breathing Blaise
4. Fire Breathing Remy
5. Fire Breathing Armand
6. Fire Breathing Ovide

———

RANCHER BEARS

When the patriarch of the Long family dies, he leaves a will that has each of his five son's scrambling to find a mate. Underneath it all, they find that family is what matters most.

1. Rancher Bear's Baby
2. Rancher Bear's Mail Order Mate
3. Rancher Bear's Surprise Package
4. Rancher Bear's Secret
5. Rancher Bear's Desire
6. Rancher Bears' Merry Christmas

Rancher Bears Complete Box Set

———

KODIAK ISLAND SHIFTERS

On Port Ursa in Kodiak Island Alaska, the Sterling brothers are kind of a big deal.
They own a nationwide chain of outfitter retail stores that they grew from their father's little backwoods camping supply shop.
The only thing missing from the hot bear shifters' lives are mates! But, not for long...

1. Billionaire Bear's Bride (COLTON)
2. The Bear's Flamingo Bride (WYATT)
3. Military Bear's Mate (TUCKER)

———

SHIFTERS OF DENVER

Nathan: Billionaire Bear- A matchmaker meets her match.
Byron: Heartbreaker Bear- A sexy heartbreaker with eyes for just one
woman.
Xavier: Bad Bear - She's a good girl. He's a bad bear.

1. Nathan: Billionaire Bear
2. Byron: Heartbreaker Bear
3. Xavier: Bad Bear

Shifters of Denver Complete Box Set

Printed in Great Britain
by Amazon

37841288R10076